THE LONG REACH

Susan Davis

Q.E.D. Press
Fort Bragg, California

THE LONG REACH
Copyright © 1993 Susan Davis

Q.E.D. Press
155 Cypress Street
Fort Bragg, CA 95437
(707) 964-9520

Cover art, "Blue Wind," pastel and gouache, 42" by 30"
copyright © 1987 Erica Fielder

Q.E.D. Press would like to thank the following people for their support and expertise: Neva Beach, Quan Tracy Cherry, Karin Faulkner, Erica Fielder, Sal Glynn, Chuck Hathaway and Noliwe Rooks; we would like to especially acknowledge publicist Belvie Rooks for her guidance and assistance, and for introducing us to Susan Davis.

ISBN No. 0-936609-27-3

Library of Congress No. 92-50343

Printed in the United States of America

10 9 8 7 6 5 4 3 2 1

To Mark

The Long Reach

The Players

One

I awoke that morning from another of the dreams: I had been bothered recently by recurring dreams of struggling through a forest with thick undergrowth. This time I passed through a stretch of mud, and when I came out I saw that there were leeches all over my calves and ankles. I waited to feel what I imagined the bite of a leech to be, but nothing happened: they just felt like snails. I couldn't brush them off with my hands, but even after I started scraping them off with some twigs it was useless because there were always more on different parts of my body.

This dream, as always, left a layer of sadness and futility over everything when I woke up. I felt like a failure when I couldn't even dream well, when I woke up already feeling tired and angry.

I pulled on my robe and went over to the window. The view was an accomplishment: I had earned it with vigilance and patience, and the spires of the City in the distance were beautiful in the early light. It was as if I could begin to breathe as I focused on them. True, they represented almost all I hated in the world: exclusion, repression, materialism. But I had worked out this much of a truce with myself: I could enjoy them for this one moment of the day if I fought the good fight the rest of the time. After spending the extra time at the window, I had to hurry to catch my bus. I almost knocked over the water jug but saved it with a neat catch. It's not that water's scarce outside the City, it's just that it has to be carried home from the big public faucets. So it might as well be scarce. Anyway I took my catch as a good omen for the rest of the day: things might be touch and go, but they'd come out in the end.

No matter how cold the water was (and it wasn't bad in early October), no matter how reluctantly I plunged my hands in and splashed them up to my face that first time, I was always glad I'd done it by the time I dried off, because it was refreshing and I liked feeling clean.

The morning went on like any other. Warming up as I dressed, eating a cold breakfast. I didn't pack a lunch because Paul, my boss, had been treating me every day. Sandwiches or chicken or driving out with him for something hot, I was just like a little Pavlov's dog for those lunches. And they were even better of course because Paul never made any demands on me, never exacted a toll of any kind. I was still a little suspicious of him, with his being an Insider, but I enjoyed those lunches.

I went down the stairs and outdoors; the morning was very quiet. I didn't sense any trouble anywhere. Having grown up Outside, I didn't usually notice the way things looked. The trash everywhere, all the relics of destruction and abandonment, things broken or leaning or decaying. Browns and grays and dirty yellows were easy to skim over while the eyes looked for something interesting or pertinent to survival, like movement. But on bad days, days with bad dreams, like this one, the dirt came at my eyes a little more insistently. I tried to leash them and keep them still, keep them from seeking out the darkest interiors on each side of the street, as if asking, is this it? Is this the worst thing I could see?

I got a seat on the bus and settled in for the slow hour's crawl. With all my rebelliousness, I have to admit that the daily rhythms of getting up at a certain time, then napping on the bus, then working, then doing what I wanted to in the evenings, soothed me in a way. I had always worked. I had had the brains to rise above the hardest jobs, once my "character" was proven. It was always a funny thing about my personality that with all the dreaming and scheming and complaining I did at night, I could hold my tongue so well during the day. Between my friends and myself, we each had a part to play, and that was mine: to work, to bring City money to the Outside, to be a link between my friends and the City. Many times I wished I could hang out with them all day, talking terrorism and playing around, but when I tried that I just got bored and restless, so I worked. In return they were the family I could dip in and out of, close-knit and very warm, really kind of happy, at least with each other. They ended up with more than the government Subsistence, I avoided isolation. It balances like that in the Outside.

A couple of rows up, a City brothel recruiter was sweet-talking a couple of young girls. When he finished with them he made his way back in my direction, keeping an eye out for other possibilities. He passed me right by; at thirty-two they didn't stop for me anymore. City taste is young, young, young. I'd been glad when they'd started ignoring me, although I hadn't been able to really understand why. I knew I had never known how to act when they talked to me. On the one hand, I liked them because of their subversive attitude, belittling the harmless, flabby, white-bellied old fools and talking up the easy money and easy living conditions, all of it actually mostly true. There had been times when I had enjoyed the perversity of sex-as-commodity: it was exciting to be so wanted. On the other hand, these stints had never lasted long and usually I apologized my way to freedom, ready to vomit if I was touched one more time. So I knew I would never last in a brothel, a twenty-four hour milieu, no matter how hot the water or how potent the drugs.

I thought of what Paul always said about following my thoughts to understand myself. Sometimes I thought Paul was just a touch insane, but lots of his advice worked well and he was certainly very intelligent. This was his latest theory that he wanted me to "think over," as he put it. Which really meant he wanted me to decide to believe it lock, stock and barrel just like he did, but he was too good a teacher to come out and say it like that. "Just play with it," he would say, and it was from him I'd gotten the feeling of my conscious mind being like a living thing, and therefore a little apart from me, not being exactly Me, if I could watch it play with an idea like a ball. Because that's what it did, once I asked it to: my mind would pick up this idea and peer around it and over it and see what it connected to and what came after that, and how the idea smelled and how it felt to have it around, and what happened physically around it, and after a few days, if my mind liked it, lo and behold I'm using the new idea just like I've believed it all my life, without Me ever having made a formal decision. It's like white magic.

So I leaned back and shut my eyes. My bag was tight and secure under my arms, my knees propped; this was a pleasant time of day, meditative. Why had I been so uncomfortable with the recruiters in the past? I started the chain of thought. Because...each time I had had to think of excuses, and that made me feel like a coward. Why had I had to make excuses? Because I couldn't think of an overwhelming reason why I shouldn't go. But I *knew* why now: I couldn't tolerate it emotionally, too neurotic. Maybe that was part of my discomfort: it seemed like a self-indulgent excuse. A weakness. Infantile. I admired the strong Amazons and the sweet things whose bodies were their obedient tools, as unconflicted and professional in the practice of their trade as a mechanic's hands with his engines.

So it seemed to lead back to guilt that I wasn't prostituting. I shifted position to accommodate a rather large person who squeezed down beside me, and continued thinking. What was the main advantage of prostitution over the work

I'd ended up doing all those years? Money: no other legal means could earn an Outsider more. That was a City concept, that one ought to make the most money possible, as a top priority. How had I come to believe that? That must have been one of what Paul called hidden beliefs, I thought excitedly. And he'd said I'd find them just like this, at the end of a chain. I couldn't wait to tell him, then I bit back a smile when I realized I wouldn't be able to, given the subject matter.

Guilt, how I hated it, hated finding it in myself, like an ugly old weed. But I found it over and over. I've never really understood where it all came from, why I ended up with so much that it took years of slow peeling away and discarding to get rid of it. Of course Paul has told me his theories about that too, there isn't one thing that he doesn't have a theory on.

I was getting sleepy. One guilt seemed to lead me to another, a guilt that drew me like the pull of drugs or the scene of an accident: it was dark and big and I hovered around it before looking in its eyes. It was this: listening to the recruiters, I had wanted to join. For my own pleasure! I was as bad as the customers! And how deep were this weed's roots?

I fell asleep.

The City was as beautifully ugly as ever when I got out of the bus. Like another world. Beautifully paved and clean streets, I think that's what I always saw first. Everything orderly and just right. People's hair expensively coiffed in the latest "casual" style. Fashions almost always travel from the Outside inward; Outsiders have little choice but to be "natural" and "casual!" The reasons everyone can always tell the difference between an Insider and an Outsider (unless they're deliberately cross-dressing) are the quality of the cloth, the dirt Outsiders sometimes have to be casual about, and the comparatively lesser facial tension of the Insiders. Most of the time Insiders have relatively little to worry about. For

Outsiders, it seems there's always something to worry about: bad food, illness, cold, heat, toxics, things not working, things falling apart, being attacked, getting shot for committing a crime or for being suspected. Interrogation. The first time Paul went on about my having control over these things through my beliefs and desires, I got upset and kind of huffy, the way I get when I have a lot to say but I'm too scared to say it. He apologized and said he didn't mean to say I wasn't up against a lot, and then he actually sat there while I shouted for several minutes about conditions on the Outside, very indignant and I must say rather eloquent, but foolishly hot-headed. He had the most sympathetic look on his face; then I'd exhausted myself and felt bad since he had been so kind to me, and I apologized to *him*. That was the first time I got a real hint of what kind of person Paul is.

For a period of time before I went to work for him, I walked around with such anger that Insiders seemed like donkeys or dogs on their hind legs, or like birds I've seen in pictures with clumps of brown grass on their heads, some kind of adornment the opposite sex was just wild about. Knowing Paul humanized them again, although they were still the enemy.

I tried to be unobtrusive when I went into the shop. It was always so quiet and Paul usually so engrossed in something or other that I was self-conscious about my coarse Outsiderness. I tried to glide delicately to my desk, to move gracefully and quietly, but he looked up and greeted me as he always did, with a smile: "Good morning, my dear, and how are you?"

Every day I was so reassured that I kind of smirked when I answered, "Fine, thanks, Paul, and you?" I never knew whether he had caught on that I was paranoid and so liked the reassuring sound of it.

"Very well, very well," he said today. "Those Chaucer texts finally came in, by messenger, can you imagine?" We always laughed at the ways Insiders could devise of wasting money.

I don't know what I expected—for him to look up, his eyes cold? having suddenly realized overnight that my darkness, my coarse black clothing, my moods, were boring or repulsive? Later in the day I would marvel at how anxious I was when I came in, but every morning was the same.

"And how were your dreams last night then?" he asked today.

I made a face. "Oh, just another forest dream, stupid things. Only this time I was attacked by a bunch of toothless leeches, ugh."

He made a face, too. "What was that all about?"

"Oh, I don't know," I said. I was impatient. He always thought dreams meant something. "I don't understand what any of them mean, I mean what, that I'm trapped or something? Well sure, I was born Outside, so I'll always be trapped, so why do I start having these all of a sudden? There's no way out and that's the end of it."

He didn't say anything so I looked at him, and he was sitting there like an idiot, very serious-faced, but definitely laughing at me inside. I heard my last words again and had to laugh too. "Okay, okay, what I mean is, what would be the purpose of point out the obvious and—stirring up these feelings if there's no solution anyway?"

"Ah, well, solutions, there's a different story. They wouldn't be dreams if they were merely conscious, rational solutions, would they?"

I looked at him for a while until I realized he was finished. "So, what's the point?'

"Ha! They're your dreams, my dear, I'm sure you know better than I!" and he went back to his work.

He could be irritating. I saw that I'd messed up the sorting and I stacked the papers to begin again. He'd led me right down the garden path and then just left me hanging, but I seemed to fall for it every time.

"All right," I said. I felt some determination this morning. "So what if I took a huge machete with me and just tore away at the undergrowth?"

"What would that do about the leeches? Still—" before I could answer—"why don't you suggest that to yourself and see what happens?"

"Yeah, but so what if I did? So what if I cleared the whole damned forest? I'd still wake up in the real world, in the same situation!" My blood rose a little. This was my theme, and I played it well.

"Would you indeed?"

Was that a contradiction? or not? He said it almost as if he were curious; it was hard to keep arguing with such a marshmallow.

"I just wish they'd stop. Good dreams serve a better purpose; at least they give you something nice to think about the rest of the day."

"That they do, that they do."

Seeing him preoccupied, I settled in and did some work myself. After a few minutes I got paranoid again. What if my stupid coarse ways had irritated him?—he must be revolted. Silence would be best, but then I had to find out.

"Are the texts as interesting as you'd hoped?"

"Oh, yes, yes, come here a moment. Now look here at this original text, this section right here. Here I've written out a translation, and now here's the traditional translation." He started going on like he always did, not that I wasn't interested. I was relieved because I knew then that he hadn't been feeling cool toward me, he'd only been wrapped up in this Chaucer.

It was fun standing so close to him. I surreptitiously looked over his fading gray hair, his broad brown fingers, the whole barrel-like mass of him. I have a good feel for people and he felt healthy, more balanced than Insiders usually did. The times when we kicked off work and played around with some book or old manuscript, it was like the specters of past and future hung outside the windows and I could simply ignore them.

I didn't believe much in unseen forces, but I didn't see the harm in occasionally letting go of little misty bursts of gratitude for working there. The shop was a continually astounding playground—for both of us! Like an ant-farm or catacomb, there were all kinds of passageways and levels, and the material forming them was mostly wood and stone. There were chambers, garrets, studies, dens, libraries and parlors. Many shelves stuffed with printed material, mostly from the previous two centuries, some older. Reading was out of fashion and it seemed to me that papers and books and folios of all kinds from all over the world were on their way here, battered and exhausted, to die. But we treasured them, we tenderly read what they had to say, their sole reason for existence leaping out at us onc last time before, possibly, crumbling apart. People could buy, borrow or browse, and of course sell too.

I never really got used to Paul's way of doing business. He never advertised and he frankly didn't care how much money he made. I knew that he had no material need to do so, still it was so against the times! People didn't notice the place, and when they did, often I would watch them come in and wander around with a puzzled look on their faces and then leave. They didn't know what to make of it! And of course Paul may not have even noticed they'd been there at all, and I'd be laughing—it was amazing! People liked cement and electronics, and the wood and paper seemed dirty to them, I could see it in their stiff, careful movements as they handled the books, or had to touch a shelf.

Sometimes Paul would gently imitate and mock people behind their backs, the silliest ones. Sometimes he said things about the obnoxious ones that I never knew Insiders said about each other. He wouldn't sell things he liked if he knew they were being bought for appearance's sake, a book-shelf or table decoration. He made up prices on the spot. Customers would be put off by his persistent interrogations about their intentions for one of his favorites.

Sometimes I would feel embarrassed for him: I knew that part of his stubbornness was age, the way the old seem to be parting with parts of themselves with their possessions. I would think of his wife, recently dead, and feel sad for him, but then I'd kick myself for being such a fool. Feeling sorry for an Insider! He could have anything or practically anyone he wanted! There are agencies for every need and persuasion. Then I'd feel sad for him anyway, and back and forth. Frankly, a lot of the time when I was doing work that allowed a bit of daydreaming, I was like some kind of judge and jury, weighing this and that, and the rights and wrongs of the world, or like a computer that has taken over its own control and is endlessly, meaninglessly computing. I always ended up in the same place, but I had some nice turns of logic and posed some very persuasive, very piteous arguments to myself.

One thing I tried to avoid thinking about was what would change if he did take a woman; I was afraid he would get all quiet and pretty much ignore me. The worst would be if he took off with her and closed the shop, for obvious reasons. Or brought her in, if she was smart and interested in all this stuff, which she probably would be. I didn't think he'd let me go just like that if that happened. If I got the chance I'd try to get in good with her, make myself indispensable, then hopefully they'd find enough work for me to stay on. But no matter how cleverly I arranged things mentally, the fact was I felt I had no control over any of it and sometimes I really upset myself just imagining being kicked out, dwelling on the details, like a fool.

It was just before closing that this City official came around. He must have been there a few minutes, talking with Paul, when I came into the room and went to my desk. He sat casually facing Paul across his desk, one of those thick-faced Teutonic types, so different from the brown open faces and quick eyes of most of my friends. I disliked him right away.

"So I gather then that your little place here has experienced few security problems?" the official asked.

"Fortunately that is true," Paul answered. "There is little

here of use on the black market." He was playing it up well, real smooth.

The official got up and walked slowly around, looking at our books. "There is nothing that is of no use on the black market. Nothing, that is, that's of use on a legitimate market as well," and when he said that, he had the meanest little smile on his face; I just hoped Paul didn't see it.

He picked up a little brown volume. The gold lettering was almost worn away. "What, for example, would this sell for?"

Paul got up and went over to him. "That, my good man, is a volume of Wordsworth, a minor poet of the 19th century. Its worth is negligible, but if it suits your fancy, it is yours."

It took a couple of moments, but then I understood. If Paul had shared the enthusiasm he really felt, the official would surely have just confiscated the book. Even an Insider doesn't deny the City its desires. To simply deny value in the book might have made the official suspicious, and he might have demanded it out of spite. But the way Paul so blandly offered it while denying its value ought to do the trick.

The official opened the book and looked through it a little. He smiled and then laughed. "I can see why you said he was minor: most of these don't rhyme, and the ones that do are so long-winded you can't be bothered to finish them. Here, old man, junk like this isn't fit for a gift for a fiancee, is it?" and he tossed the volume on a shelf. I was amused and relieved and I knew Paul was too.

The official picked up another volume. "And here, 'Chopin,'" he pronounced like the verb, "what's this, a collection of folk tunes for 'choppin' wood?"

Maybe I was remembering an encounter I had had with one of Paul's friends the day before, which had been awkward but generally easier than I'd expected. Maybe I was overconfident from an especially happy and prideful day, or just struck by the humor of his arrogance, but I let out some kind of a little smirk of laughter. Right away he looked at me, and then it was like a kind of electric, instant understanding in the air: the official knew that I was laughing at him and not at his jokes, and I knew that although he was uneducated, he was smart. Real smart. Then to top it off I felt my face flush. I couldn't believe how my body would betray me. I had completely fumbled and lost control of the situation in a few seconds.

Sure enough, he walked slowly over, leafing through the music as he came. I kept my eyes down.

"I see you have an Outsider assisting you here."

"Yes, some two months now," Paul said, bless him, as if nothing were wrong.

"Any trouble with her?"

"None, sir. However, you know the bright ones...well, sometimes they can be a bit...eccentric, you know—" His voice was perfect: slow, placating, man-to-man.

Now the official was looking at me, and his eyes really burned into me as he circled around.

"Let me give you some advice, old man. The latest research shows genetic defect among much of the Outsider population. I have quite a bit of experience with them and this one has the coarseness, the shifting eyes, the..." and he leaned closer and sniffed "...odor, that suggest many generations squatting in fields, swatting flies, et cetera, et cetera, no matter how superficially intelligent."

"I shall take that under advisement."

Then he was looking back at the music. I wanted so much for that to mean the end of it; he knew I was scared, if only that were all he wanted. But not so.

"So, Outsider, you find my cultural ignorance amusing?"

What was I to say to that? I couldn't think of anything except the obvious. I just started stuttering, "No, no, of course not, sir...I...was laughing because...I have often myself found such a silly collection of...chopping songs...to be amus-"

"Have you?"

Where was the trap? I could smell one but I couldn't figure it out. I just stuttered more.

"Read this aloud," he said.

I took the book he handed me and it shook as I read it. "Frederick Chopin, one of the foremost composers of the 19th cent—"

"Ah, so they are not a collection of chopping songs?"

"I thought it was...another volume you were looking at, sir—"

He turned triumphantly to Paul. "You see? I've been here just a few minutes and already she's been insolent and she has lied."

I was so desperate. "There is really another book that contains—" and then he rapped his fingers across my mouth very lightly, just symbolic of things to come, really, but the suddenness of the gesture spooked me and I jumped about a mile, then backed up against the wall.

"No more from you," he said casually.

"My dear sir," Paul said, "I most regret this unfortunate occurrence," and I heard him coming toward us. "As I said, she is bright and I have had to discipline her in just such a way several times myself—"

"Then I'll relieve you of her at once."

"Ah, that is of course your prerogative, sir, however may I beg your ear, just for a moment, ah, there are extenuating circumstances, so to speak, if I could just speak with you for a very brief moment—" all this while he pulled me together as if he were totally exasperated with me. He made it clear I could and should get lost, and then he turned to speak to the official.

In the lavatory I just let the tears flow with the water. Almost everyone needs to cry after such an encounter, it was best not to fight it.

My mind was spinning in some high, only partly efficient gear. I was really stirred up now, and I thought of my friends, and of how I would probably join a gang and die soon, now that my work record was probably ruined. They had always encouraged me to do this, and now I had a personal grudge to settle.

I shut off the water and pulled my knife out from under my dress. I heard laughter, then Paul's voice, then laughter again. It made my skin crawl. Was he betraying me? OF COURSE! an inner voice shouted. Risk his beautiful shop for an Outsider? He would do what he had to, and so would I. The voices grew faint. Something about the cadences told me the conversation was ending. I got in position behind the half-opened door.

Footsteps. One set or two? I crouched, and when the door opened I was ready—but it was only Paul. We froze for a moment, his hand raised involuntarily, me unable to release until I knew I was safe.

He moved his hand in a little pacifying gesture. "Laura, Laura, he's gone, you're safe, my dear, please...all is well..." he just kept saying, until I came out of the little spell I was under and, after checking over his shoulder, and now really not knowing what to do, I tossed my knife aside. I was relieved but felt foolish too.

"Come then, come with me and let's talk a while," he went on, and took my hand. I felt like running, hitting him, shouting, crying, and I did nothing. I just let him lead me into the hall.

"My, my, who would have guessed that such a pleasant day would have ended in such an ordeal?" I knew he didn't expect an answer, he was only starting on one of his digressions. I was glad; I couldn't have spoken anyway. We were moving along now and I was almost curious as to where we were going, but not quite. "What's called for now is a nice cup of tea, laced with a touch of something stronger, I should think. Do you remember those Victorian novels when the heroine would have a shock of some kind, probably see her husband naked or some such outrage, and fall into a 'swoon' they called it, and someone, usually the housekeeper, would give her a little shot of brandy or some tea with rum? Of course, it was no wonder they swooned so often, with those corsets made of what—dolphin bones or some such—"

"Whale bones," I said, incredibly enough.

"Whale bones, of course! That's an odd thing if you think about it, isn't it? Wearing a whale's bones for beauty! And yet how judgmental those Victorians were regarding the eccentricities of personal adornment of the indigenous peoples they encountered around the world. Savages, they called them. Ah well, this is one of the larger flaws in the thinking of the western peoples. Although truth to tell, many peoples of all persuasions use one word for themselves, meaning 'The People' and another for other humans, so perhaps it's a universal trait, after all."

I knew what he was up to. It was the same thing Mother Dhia did when someone went to her half-crazy with some problem. She would cluck around you and just ramble quietly and slowly on about other things, and by the time you had the sense to wonder what she was talking about, you were automatically feeling better. That was okay. If he wanted to give me a chance to get myself together before going out into the street, I would be appreciative. I knew I probably wouldn't see him again, anyway, which was a sad thing.

We went into the velvet parlor, and he seated me on an old velvet chair. I was touched at what he was trying to do for me, and all my anger was seeping away into the woman's realm of tears. To cry would be too much, though, so I just sat and tried to calm down while he was gone for the tea.

"That's the way, my dear, just rest yourself," he said when he came back. When I opened my eyes it seemed like reality had shifted; at least, I had shifted my weight in my body and seemed to feel more comfortable in it. He had the sweetest old silver tea service with him, and the aroma that hit me a couple of seconds later was one that had always filled me with the most foolish, sentimental notions (he knew that). As I breathed in, it seemed my other senses opened and I saw the warm colors and heard the silence, felt how special was the relationship I had with this room. Paul sat back and closed his eyes, sipping his cup, and I managed to wrench myself out of my self-absorption long enough to notice how weary he was.

I would expand to the occasion: I would be noble. "I know what you have to say to me, Paul, and it's all right, honestly."

"Ha. I should be a bit surprised if you did, since I'm not quite sure myself, my dear. Still, you never know. What would you have me say?"

What did he mean, he didn't know? How could we possibly go on working together, after this? I had displayed all my worst attributes, coincidentally attributes that could cause him the most trouble: I was a lightning rod for trouble with authority, always had been and, judging from today, always would be. Moreover, he had seen me reduced to my true animal status, where before we could play at forgetting that. But all that, that was too much to go into; it was sickening. He must just be too kindhearted to bring himself to say it, I decided again. So I had to find a civilized way to say it. He had been so kind, I didn't mind the effort. "I...won't be in tomorrow." I was furious when my throat choked off the last syllable; it would look like I was begging!

"Is that what you want?" The way he asked it, I couldn't tell what he wanted. Was he relieved, or disappointed, or what?

I cleared my throat. "Don't you think that's best?"

"Best for whom?"

"I guess...for you."

"For me? Why is that do you think?"

I couldn't help it; I glanced at the ceiling. "I don't want to bring any further trouble to you." I was sincere about that.

"I appreciate that; at my age, it's rather exhausting."

Well, then I had to laugh, and he did too.

"I don't seem to be able to help getting into trouble, though..."

"Well, I don't know, you seem to have handled yourself well enough these past few months, that's many days compared to this one, true enough?"

I had to admit this was true. Leave it to him to see it that way, of all ways. I just couldn't yet believe that he would actually just give me a little lecture and let it go.

"I...meant no harm..."

"Hm...I don't know, Laura...I don't think I would have wanted to be in the alley in which you caught him unawares..."

This time he knew he had me; he knew I would be proud that he remembered my MO, when I had only mentioned it once. I suddenly felt like a friendly tiger, but at last some sensible part of me kept my mouth shut until I could talk civilized again.

"I mean," I said, "I didn't—start anything." What a foolish sentence! Like a child in a foolish playground dispute! But what I felt was 'Please say I'm right!'

"Oh, the man was a pig, a positive swine in attributes, actually sort of a...pig in wolf's clothing, how's that for a description? And yet a man for all that, so mortified and cowed by the beauty, intellect and scorn of a mere waif from the Wastelands that within minutes of her arrival in his presence he was reduced to infantile rage. I tell you it was like watching lovers, or dancers, the way you touched each others' most intimate fears and scars, bending and swaying to an ancient rhythm indeed."

I was shocked right out of my little dream. What he was implying—no, saying outright—! And then as I puffed up, he really seemed to hook into that. I knew he liked getting a reaction from me, but he'd gone too far. "Those words are insane!"

"Are they?" Just like that, "Are they?"

"You talk as if—I participated in—as if I brought it on—"

"I'm not saying you did so deliberately, nor that you deserved it, nor that it is what must be." It was as if he'd been waving his arms to get my attention, or like I'd been asleep, and now that he'd gotten it, he took off. I wanted to trip him up, so I listened to every word. "It is as if you have a beacon, a broadcast signal, and due to an accumulation of experiences and beliefs you advertise, like a neon sign in the night, 'Look here! I am a warrior, a rebel, I am an Outsider but I will wage a most satisfactory fight for anyone who cares for such things. Exorcise your demons here! All who see me try to hurt me, it is my strange and sad fate.'"

I was getting white-hot now, so hot I was cold. "Why on earth would I do that?"

He got up and went to look out the window. I was pleased that I had hurt him a little. "I know you feel as if the answer, and indeed, the question were foreign to you, but I assure you that both are more accessible to you than to me." I waited when he paused.

"Growing up, as you did, being cared for generally by a group, is not in and of itself harmful. From what you have told me you received as much food, material necessities, even affection and support as any other average...Outsider." He paused again. "It is, however, as if a rosebush grew among brambles and other plants, growing a thick coat of thorns itself, ever striving toward the sun, ever awaiting the moment when it will have the room, the nurturing, the...peace, if you will, to blossom, to show its true nature, so to speak." He was still facing the window, and he raised his hand to his mouth and cleared his throat softly.

"My friends aren't brambles; I'm not superior to them."

"Is a rose superior to a bramble? Certainly not. The bramble has strength, vitality, produces berries of variety and exquisite plumpness, an ecstasy to the tongue and the guts. They grow in great arcs, exuberantly carving out their space in the general scheme of things. Seen from this point of view, the rose is actually rather useless, do you see?" When he looked at me this time, I had to smile.

"The rose is merely different; of course it's not really useless. When was the last time you saw a cluster of brambles gathered in a fine glass vase, berries and all? The purpose of a rose in a vase may be more difficult to describe in words, yet you know inside that its purpose is as valid as that of the bramble." When he stopped to look at me after saying this, it was like something knotting and unknotting inside my stomach.

"Now say we add a complication. The rose sees over a wall that separates our fine, wild brambles from...let us say a fine lawn of grass. The grass is soft, even, as sturdy in its way as the brambles, as cultivated as the rose. But the rose sees how easy life is for the grass, how each blade seems to conform to its neighbors, how it never seems to reach much beyond a certain height, and compares it to the pinched, unreliable, undernourishing conditions under which the brambles must grow; to the rose, the grass seems weak, self-satisfied, dull, and the rose admires the brambles for their strength and independence. Our rose therefore continues to strive to emulate its companions, growing quickly, sharpening its thorns and toughening its stems, delaying any hint of blossom, for deep down it has begun to believe that the red softness it feels within itself is reminiscent of the hated grass: effete, weak, self-indulgent, unfairly advantaged, and somehow a betrayal of its friends the brambles.

"And so our rose looks around and sees no one like itself, for its existence is by now rooted in self-denial. It feels itself a hybrid, an anomaly, hopelessly and fatally flawed. In its darkest hours, it wishes simply to wither and bend to the dust, to be no more, and yet its own brand of vitality, delicate or not, prevents this. To die for the sake of its friends is an appealing idea, for the expiation of guilt afforded, guilt over that red velvet flaw it senses within itself, guilt for the inexplicable yearning it feels for the other blossoms it sees waving and bobbing in the distance. Those visions, those dreams of thrilling color and variety, are condemned as weak, as of the enemy, by the rose, and yet its attention is continually drawn there against its will, further feeding the cyclic spiral of guilt and yearning.

"Can you accept anything that I'm saying?"

He already could see that the words were burned in my mind, but acceptance? "What kind of...solution would there be...?"

"A very fine question, the very same as I should myself ask. Supposing a little funny gardener came by, and just happening to see the fine outlines and curves of this rose—" and he gave me a broad wink—"simply clears a little space on his side of the wall—the grassy side, for our gardener is rather faint-hearted and would be frightened to venture to the other side—and invites the rose to sprout anew there, to grow as it would. Not too far from the wall, so that it could mingle with its friends the brambles if it wished, but in the free, clear, safe space of the—Inside, if you will. Moreover, the gardener would encourage the rose to be fanciful, frivolous, would care for and flatter that exquisite, red splendor until it burst up through the stem into the world. My guess, by the way, is that the grass would be mortified at this shameless extravagance, but that the old friends the brambles would stare in unaffected pleasure and wonder, for their love for the rose is genuine."

Then he stopped and I realized he was done. I guess I began to love him then, because I understood how he felt about what he thought he saw in me. But this wasn't a situation that could be handled in the usual way. I had to try, for once in my life, to be delicate too. I got up and went over to him, where he was still looking out the window.

He clicked his tongue. "I'm not pleased with the analogy, it has genetic connotations I didn't intend. All I'm trying to say in my horribly rambling way," he said, turning to me, "is that you might try to alter that signal, that inner stance that others do perceive even as we see the lights over there at night. That you...play with the feeling that you are safe, that you have a haven here, but more importantly, that your haven moves with you because it is in you. It resides in a deep knowledge of the innate worth of yourself, no matter how unusual a form that may take. Others *will respond* to this."

He knew me so well, did he know that I was just about beyond listening by then? "Listening to you..." I tried to start, and faded off. I just couldn't talk, I couldn't yet connect what I felt to the part of me that spoke. "All I know is, thank you, and I...really want to try." I watched my finger skim back and forth across the table. "I've never felt that you're like...the others, and...if there were a way to...repay you...but that's not the word I mean...I would...consider myself honored...although it's probably incredibly presumptuous of me—" and then I watched his hand close over mine; I kept my eyes there in some kind of sudden terror.

"Allow me to clarify, my dutiful friend, that I meant only for you to continue your employment as my assistant here in this shop, although should you find it necessary to fling yourself at me in a violent outburst of passion someday, I cannot promise that I would be able to successfully resist my own response." Then I had to laugh, and so did he, and suddenly things were the same as they'd been before, only, of course, better.

I found I could talk again. "I'm going to think about what you said. Right now it feels like my head's just stuffed full, but—"

"Ah, that's the unfortunate effect of too close association with me, I do that to all my friends. Be sure to keep your wits about you on your way home, don't bump into any doorways."

"I won't. Um, about...that man—"

"He probably will be no trouble. I'm afraid I had to tarnish our reputations, but it was all I could think of at the time and it did seem to prove effective. I shall refrain from going into detail unless you wish me to."

I didn't—I understood. Some kind of mistress thing had been a good way to explain and handle it.

Some two hours later I was waiting at my stop. There were not many people so late, but it was too early to be deserted yet, so I was pretty much at ease. I was very tired. I'd spent the two hours at the shops looking for a present for Paul, just a little something. I hadn't really been to those shops in years: the cool, rude looks of the clerks and the Insider customers, the frustration at the prices, mostly the knowledge of the exploitation behind each trinket and dress had kept me away. It hardly matters that Outsiders have free movement in the City, when it's made so uncomfortable for us everywhere. But today I wanted to see all the pretty things.

I hadn't found anything for Paul. I had, but I would have had to steal it and he would have known and it would have been very awkward. It wouldn't have been a problem if he had been an Outsider but...that wasn't the case, and I figured I might as well try to face it. He wasn't an Outsider and—I loved him, in a way at least; I threw the two concepts together and let them fight it out.

I had my sketches at home, but I couldn't use them, the paper was too cheap. I thought of a frame, and still ended up doing nothing. I was feeling pretty jittery.

I'd seen roses everywhere, patterned in fabrics, on pottery, big splashes on dresses and tiny prints on book jackets. Each time I saw one I seemed to feel him stroke my heart. If he were an Outsider, I thought I would know better what to do as well as what to buy. I felt very brave and rough, and I forgot about how scared I'd been when he'd touched my hand. I'd been having sex since I was very young, under many different kinds of conditions, and it was pretty inconceivable that I would be scared to have it with Paul. I just wanted to figure out the right time, the right way, because every time we were close enough it just...felt awkward to me; I couldn't smooth the way for both of us like I was used to doing with others.

I knew that part of the reason was that I wasn't sure that I hadn't misread him after all, that he really meant to stay at a level of friendship. This made a lot of sense when I switched to a more objective way of thinking: I was aging, I had all these flaws plus of course being across the Line, whereas he had the choice of so very many, as refined and as wealthy as himself.

When he pulled up at the stop I laughed, it was so much like a dream. He really did seem surprised to see me, and said he had just finished dinner with a friend, could he give me a lift? I said okay, only as far as the Wall stop. There never could be reason enough to risk his venturing beyond there.

I loved driving with him: he went so fast. Faces and lights shot by, but in my memories, they are motionless snapshots.

He said he was heading for the Baths, would I like to come?

I said I couldn't, I had to get home.

He said he knew it was a shameless indulgence but he so loved the warm, swirling waters. He threatened to give me a gift coupon some day so I could go on my own. I thanked him.

When we pulled up at the Wall I sat and watched an image of myself open the door and get out, over and over. He waited.

Finally I had to do something; I had to decide what I wanted. What I found myself doing was asking him if he'd mind if I changed my mind, and he said he didn't.

At the Baths the water made both of us sleepy and emotional in no time. I hugged the wall, and he touched my back so softly, and asked how I was, and I gave up then and started to cry—I was feeling so many emotions, not all pleasant. When I leaned up against him he held me so gently, and he didn't question me or comfort me or get upset, I just felt him all around me. Then I knew there was something on his mind, so I asked him, and he was all choked up and hesitant at first, just like I'd been, and he finally confessed that he'd been developing this fear as he entered his fifties that he'd seem ridiculous as a man, especially with a younger woman. This was something I knew about, and my heart melted and for once in my life I managed to be delicate and poetic and told him that when I was with him I liked being able to see his younger self and his older self in his face, because I knew that he had kept them a part of him instead of just projecting them onto me and chasing me around all desperate and foolish. I said that being with him was exciting because it was like being with several men at once, in that way, and that made him laugh, and I knew he believed me.

And...there were other ways I spoke to him, made him know the way I felt. Then there were no more obstacles between us, we had cleared them away like a farmer weeding his fields, and we could be to each other what we'd always wanted to be.

Two

When Laura first entered my shop, I could not have been more stunned had a leopard or panther stalked in, knowing it was out of place, extremely wary, its alien eyes fixing one with that legendary hypnotic effect—its eyes and its unearthly beauty. I was particularly taken with her lovely skin, a heavily-creamed coffee with a tint of charcoal just glazed over.

I had specified that I wanted an Outsider with integrity and intelligence, never mind docility or diligence. Actually there was an absolutely enormous list of qualifications I had had to go through; I had tried to turn it in with only a few checked off but they had refused to process it unless every single one was completed. Anyway they had informed me that although she had never actually been in any formal trouble, they didn't care much for her attitude, but she most fit what I had asked for, and to let them know if I wasn't pleased and they would send another, etc. etc. Dealing with them had resembled dealing with people of other countries. I was always a little uncertain of the vocabulary and nuances of communication, but I was sure at a glance that Laura was indeed what they had said she was. To use the despicable Insider terminology, "domestic but not tame."

I'm afraid I did nothing to decrease her inherent paranoia as she crossed the room to my desk: as I said I was taken off guard and I simply watched. After her initial stabbing glance into my eyes, she kept hers lowered as she came across the room, until she reached me and presented her papers, when she raised them briefly again with what I knew she hoped passed for a smile, actually a small grimace. Of course I was drinking in many impressions at once at that point: the dampness of the papers she gave me and her surreptitious wiping of her hands on her dress afterward; the coarseness of her black clothing, but also the way it was shaped to fit her beautiful form appealingly, even trimmed with some sweet material; the tension that stiffened her shoulders and drew her spirit down around her like a mourning shawl; and, above all, the bottled rage that rose up through her throat and was checked with effort at the doors of her eyes and her lips, etched from long practice. I was aware that she saw not me, but some kind of clothed and daylit demon.

Well, now I was somewhat at a loss. I am quite a coward, really, when it comes to confrontations and the like. What was I to do? On the one hand I liked her immediately, not only for her beauty, but because I was intrigued and because, being somewhat of a spiritualist, I felt I recognized her in that way. Yet, on the other hand, I certainly didn't like the idea of working side by side with a seething volcano, day in and day out.

"Well, my dear," I said, mustering up some bonhomie, "it is a pleasure to meet you." I offered my hand and she grasped it firmly, seeming to like the gesture, relaxing just a bit with a little exhalation of breath and a slightly more genuine grimace-smile.

"Thank you for the opportunity," she replied quietly, in such beautifully low tones, with the slightest, most elusive Hispanic accent, more a lilt or a lisp really, that I knew it would be hopeless for me to try to force myself to reject her, at least right away.

"Not at all, not at all, you've evidently quite earned this—opportunity," I said, glancing around the room and smiling at the last word, making a sort of joke out of it.

She grimace-smiled again, glancing around as well, unsure of what I meant. Her face was so closed, it was hard to read, but at least there seemed to be no distaste at the quite disordered situation surrounding us. That was a good sign, since I didn't want any kind of compulsively neat person rushing around constantly straightening and polishing, and finding it an easy transition into nagging me about it.

"Why don't we come along and take a tour of the place, eh?" I said, moving around from behind the desk. This was a good move, because I think we both relaxed with our attention directed anywhere but each other.

"Here is your desk, you can put your things there, and I do hope you'll find it satisfactory. I know it's old and a bit battered, and of course I could have it replaced if you find it too disagreeable, but I kept it around because—well you see it belonged to my wife, my late wife, that is, you see and I guess I've just—well, grown attached..."

"No, it's quite beautiful," she interrupted unexpectedly. Her words were still quiet and bitten back, but she touched the desk in a gesture that was at once protective, respectful, and honestly appreciative of its old beauty. Now she looked directly into my eyes, for one of those wonderfully timeless moments. Seeing her there, much as I'd tried to prepare for this moment, I had felt so uncomfortable—a new person, one I'd have to see day in and day out, learn her habits, tolerate her moods; but above all, there was the fact of her not being my wife, with whom I had felt so comfortable, so happy, all the years of our marriage...I cannot describe the reassurance and the knowing behind that gesture of Laura's. Somehow the enormous discomfort we both felt was briefly swallowed in that moment, as into a deep dark pool, with the ripples of its disappearance fading quickly and leaving no trace.

"It is, actually, quite a fine thing," I said gratefully, touching the spot her fingers had brushed. I started cataloging its make and characteristics in the way that's automatic for me, moving on around the room with her and off into the rest of the shop.

I tended, as I always do, to continually digress into narratives about beloved pieces we came across, forgetting most of the time that I was supposed to be training her for her work there. It was quite amazing, we actually found an authentic, positively ancient harpsichord, of course fallen into disrepair, but exuding a magical aura of other times and places nevertheless. Naturally I was leery of her touching it, since she had a sort of reined-in forcefulness about her that made her not the most graceful of people. But, for once that day taking an independent action, she approached it, seemingly fascinated, and it seemed that all the random energy careening about within her focused to a series of slow, deliberate gentle motions as she took up a nearby cloth and carefully smoothed away some dust from its surface. My sputtered cautions as to its age and delicacy trailed off as I watched, my eyes mesmerized by the glow of sandalwood ardently, faithfully emerging from beneath the cloth. After a few moments she stopped suddenly and with a glance at me surreptitiously put the cloth somewhere and stepped away back toward the door of the room. An odd, transparent gesture that conveyed her recovered discomfort perfectly. For surely the millionth time in my life I wished that I weren't so thin-skinned regarding the moods and feelings of others. And for not the last time with Laura I felt a sense of helplessness and indecision regarding how to deal with my feelings and how to relate to her.

That evening I pondered the situation. On the one hand I could simply adopt a cool, detached role, one already molded and pre-existent in both of our minds. Fair but disinterested, I could retreat back into the seductive array of all my books and treasures and research, and I knew she would do so comfortably as well, as casually as I knew her hair was dark and curled about her neck. I had seen her eyes reaching for and lingering on various odd artifacts and things that I showed her and that she happened upon during the course of that long first day. It was easy to perceive, since I'd had the same appetite all my life, although with Laura, due to her circumstances, it was like wafting Christmas dinner fumes under a starving man's nose. Once she was reasonably sure I was "safe" (translated for both of us: harmless old man) she would gladly and easily surrender to their allure. I knew as I projected this line out and forward in time, however, that there were underlying repercussions to this mode of behavior, ones not following such a logical, dispassionate course. For I knew myself, and my feelings toward Laura had in the course of one day already exceeded that role, and there were certain things I sensed in the feeling of her eyes on me as well. Could a hermit crab, venturing from its shell, retreat to it in its new larger size without experiencing certain constriction? True, a certain quality of trust could develop, but it would be trust based on a mutual restraint of our natural inclinations, with that restraint due to our fears.

And what a stunning labyrinth those fears formed. Archaic, voluptuous, a palace of mirrors and shadows stretching backward and forward in time, in and out of each other until the mind struggled and rebelled against exploring any further. Lost in reverie, I marveled, again not for the first nor last time, at how far to interlocked, imaginary extremes I could carry the simplest situation, and in the end my throat closed and ached for the clear eyes and loving, mocking smile of my wife.

Actually, after indulging in a few cleansing tears, I played a little game with myself that had brought me comfort in the time since Marta's death: I imagined her as vividly as possible, gave her life in my mind's eye, and, interweaving my own thoughts with a curious sort of receptivity to the image I'd created, I tried to perceive what she might have said, what her reaction would have been to the day's business.

She told me to relax (a reassuringly familiar line), and to

be my natural self. Although I was a little disappointed at the banality of this advice, it nonetheless rang true, of course, and the glint of merriment and, deeper, a sort of satisfaction in her eyes put me even more at ease. Any facade would fail with this one was a phrase that ran through my mind. And with you, of course, it concluded, with an affectionate mocking that was so characteristic of Marta that for a while I allowed myself to believe that I could feel her there with me, so warm and full that the room seemed crowded with her essence. Suddenly to my surprise I sensed the resemblance between the two women, how the lines of their psyches followed some of the same branchings, delved and probed the earth in some of the same subterranean patterns. My mind retreated back to their surface qualities, their appearances, and confirmed the accuracy of my first unconscious perception of their differentness, with my wife's lightness of color and air, her social ease and her verbal facility. Then my mind sank again to what had been revealed only after we had been together some time, how we had together discovered the deeper recesses of our natures, and I began to feel some of the resemblances again between her deeper self and that of this woman, Laura.

As it turned out, the first couple of weeks were quite pleasant. Actually we did confine our conversations largely to the work and material at hand, and a degree of trust did develop, but it was not at the expense of friendly, personal interaction either. Our interest in culture, in literature and ideas formed a ready-made bridge, quite solid and sunny, and we had many animated discussions and explorations thereon. Beneath her slow, awkward speech, which essentially never changed, was a mind of quicksilver, and she quickly learned that pretending to agree with me irked me and that I regarded it as insulting that she would think I couldn't see through it. I enjoyed her consternation as she realized I would rather become heated over a genuine disagreement than enraged over a scornful, hypocritical silence, and I would goad her into blurting out what she thought and felt, then disagree with her (sometimes for the fun of it), forcing her to assert and articulate still further, until we were having an actual dialogue and she would forget herself entirely. Of course I soon found also that she simply couldn't resist a good joke, or a bad one, for that matter, and I took delight in defusing her defensiveness with this weapon too.

This growing ease of hers was strictly limited to me, among Outsiders, and then only when we talked of neutral topics. Other topics we avoided, and other people caused Laura to draw her face down like a screen, and turn into a statue of black ice.

I came downstairs one day to find Emma Unruh pocketing change in her usual elegant, efficient manner.

"Well, Emma, and how are you today?" I asked, a string of friendly insults auditioning in my mind.

"Hello, Paul, I am in excellent health, thank you," she replied with a wide smile that actually seemed genuine, unnervingly so. She had a good one up her sleeve, no doubt.

"And what worthless trash have you sniffed out today? Old Tory speeches, perhaps? An old Grimoire, maybe?"

"Very clever, love, just remember, I pay you well for your trash."

Such good nature! "Then why do you look so goddamned happy, eh? Murdered some Picasso recently, perhaps? I heard about your caper last month, in fact, and if that's what you're so gleeful about, I might remind you that I never cared for Jaspers, myself, anyway."

"Oh...well! More's the pity. However I'm sure I'll have the chance to disturb your senile self-indulgence once more before you die. Ta-ta!" the smile never wavering.

By that time I had reached her, and my curiosity, coupled with some unnameable instinct and good bit of luck, prompted me to tweak open her bag and glimpse its contents before she could realize what was happening and clutch it closed. Comprehension chased the smiles from both our faces with a snap.

"Emma, no!"

"Too late, Paul!"

"Emma that's not fair and you know it!"

"Paul let it go, it's paid for!"

"You're not taking that anywhere!" and I seized her wrist with one hand and tugged on the bag with the other.

"Unhand me, you old bastard!" she seethed between clenched teeth.

We glared at each other for a moment.

"Emma, you know you took advantage of the girl's inexperience. Laura, give her her money back."

"On the contrary, she is far from ignorant. She knew your price and counted out every penny. The manuscript's mine!"

"Oh, Jesus!" I cried in desperation. Emma tried to take advantage by pulling on the bag, but I maintained my hold. "What is your price? I'll not take no for an answer now!"

We glared at each other again. Finally, to my relief, I saw her eyes narrow. I knew what that meant.

"Twice the price."

"Laura, what did you charge her?"

"What you...said yesterday..." Laura whispered.

I beseeched the heavens. Twice that was our take for a week.

"Give it to her," I snapped at Laura, who began fumbling in the drawer.

"And...the bust," Emma said calmly, her eyes two ice picks in my heart.

I hesitated only a moment, then, giving vent to my frustration with a roiling staccato tone, I said "Laura, get the bust of Mozart from the second floor music room." As she handed over the money and went to the stairs, Emma's claws loosened and I retrieved my treasure.

"Is that the one w—-" Laura began from the stairs.

"Christ, it's got the name carved in the bottom!" I practically shouted. I sat down wearily behind my desk and leaned back with my eyes closed until she returned and handed it over to a triumphant Emma.

"Just remember, whenever you're ready to retire..." Emma sang out, and left.

My ill temper had been tenaciously seeking a target all day; now it retrieved this one, and panting and eager, lay it at my feet.

"How could you, how could you hand over such a priceless treasure to a Philistine like Emma Unruh? What were you, in some kind of trance? Is this some kind of passive-aggressive, Outside, neo-slavery way of telling me you hate me, that you could lop off a piece of my heart and hand it over to such a person on the proverbial silver platter? Or did she bribe you—should I make you empty your pockets, I wonder? Have you no instincts, no judgment whatsoever? What did you think she planned to do with that manuscript, eh? Do you know what Emma Unruh does with priceless art, do you have any idea?" To my fevered mind, Laura's expressionless face and downcast eyes were a convenient admission of guilt. "Do you?" I shouted still louder.

"No," she whispered.

"No, you don't, do you," I said, feeling absurdly vindicated, pounding the desk in a frustration that seemed to increase as it was ventilated, for a reason about which I could not have been less curious at the moment. "But what do you do? You hand it over with a smile, without asking me, as if after two weeks you think you own the shop. Now explain that, if you can."

After a few moments she suddenly seemed to realize I actually expected a reply and cleared her throat. "I thought you were busy..."

"You thought I was busy. Too busy to know what was transpiring in my own shop. Well, you thought wrong. I don't pay you to think. I pay you to work. Don't even try to think. Do you understand? It's possible I shouldn't even have expected an—" Suddenly, finally, echoes of what I was saying were beginning to outshout the angry new words still forming in my mind. "Don't make me regret—" I revised, definitely starting to flounder. I stared at her for a few frustrated moments. "Damn you, look at me!"

She did, and naturally, the anger and fear in her eyes could not be disguised by the immobility of her face. I let her eyes finish off the tattered remains of my diatribe with a sigh. "Ah, God. Look Laura, just do this. Don't sell anything, don't even quote a price without asking me. All right? In fact, just don't even show anything old, anything valuable to anyone. Just—if you have any doubt, just send them to me. All right? Do you understand?"

"Of course," she said and lowered her eyes again. The immediacy of her reply skated over a frozen lake of other words, words I could almost hear.

I have been called a difficult man. This isn't due to some kind of repressed misanthropic streak, but actually to moods that seem to swarm over me more so than over most, a simple deep disgust at life and toward myself and all the petty limitations contained therein. Fortunately for my own balance of character I've always been surrounded by people who not only refused to tolerate much of the detritus from these moods, but who have, sometimes playfully, sometimes pointedly, poked holes in the bloated belly of my gloom, providing me with understanding of and relief from my own self.

Stewing upstairs, after the foreign but satisfying glow resulting from being able to rant and rave for once unopposed had definitely faded, its aftertaste was proving itself far less palatable. My normal perceptive faculties, it seemed, had faithfully recorded everything without need for my conscious awareness of the process, and now I grudgingly viewed flashes of Laura's pale, drawn face, the pulse pounding at her throat, saw little clips of her hands fumbling in the cash drawer. Saw those obsidian eyes. Suddenly, with red crawling up my neck and my scrotum sucking inwards, I had a feeling she might not be downstairs at all when I went down. My mind took wing then, picturing her carrying off my dearest treasures with the same controlled, tight-lipped, white-hot fury I had seen in those eyes, not to the black market, but to some place just outside the Wall, and calmly burning them all. It was this plain and ancient motive, not one more noble, that sent me trudging back downstairs.

However, when I saw her small form behind her desk as usual, the relief I felt was only partly due to this source. I was genuinely glad to see her for deeper emotional reasons that I sensed but was still too clouded to identify. The fact that she was there seemed to open up some new realm of possibility for both of us. I sensed that in some other line of probability, through a choice she had probably had to struggle to deny in this one, things had indeed ended just as I had briefly feared, a great loss to us both.

"Well, I'm glad to see you're still here," I said, surprising myself, as I approached her. It took her off guard too, I knew at once, as I saw her struggle for some reply, rejecting first one, then another, then another. After her first appraisal of me, she returned her attention to papers that I had a feeling had no more been touched than the stack of work at which I had stared for an hour upstairs. A small grimace that might have been a shrug in another lifetime was what she finally settled on, the closest thing she could dare to the rudeness of no reply.

"Let's take a break upstairs, eh? Talk a bit?" I asked, moving to the front door to lock it. When I turned, she had risen but remained where she was, rooted.

When she saw me waiting, she spoke with effort. "I—understand, you know. I won't let it happen again." Defensive, anxious.

I grimaced. "Oh, come now, that's not the issue and you know it. Come on and let's have some tea."

More emotions fighting it out. I realized she was even more scared now than if I'd said nothing. I saw her glance at the door, but in the end, she went with me.

One small room, furnished in the styles of other times, is set off from the rest of the shop. It's the one room not cluttered with papers or any other objects for the mind, but only ones for the senses. My wife and I would spend time there together in the middle of the day if we were weary or bored or, as now, to heal in times of strife. We also made love there, although it contains no bed. Fine fabrics and softness and age cover the furniture and walls. I had not entered it in the months since Marta's death, out of superstitious but natural hesitation to stir up that not-quite-healed wound that her passing had left. Within moments, though, I could tell by its dustless state that someone else had.

"I see you've discovered my little 'place away from time,'" I said when I returned with the tea, handing her a cup.

She took it from me, and sipped from it immediately although it was still quite hot. This struck me kind of tenderly, for I did the same thing in times of stress, enjoying the painful heat moving down my throat and slamming into my stomach, bringing tears to my eyes, the way some, I suppose, enjoy alcohol.

"I hope you don't mind," she said carefully. Her eyes seemed to have liquefied again—she seemed slightly more relaxed. So far so good, I thought.

I sat as well. "No, Laura, I don't mind." I took a sip of tea, trying to clear my mind so that the right words would come. "Please don't begin to censor every action or word because of what I said this afternoon."

"Begin?" she blurted, and I looked at her, saw her color rise. She looked down, and I waited. A very long minute passed, but my restraint paid off. "I always try to decide the best thing to do here," she said, a world of emotion just beneath the surface of her words.

"I know you do, Laura," I said, my voice also understated. "And you do a very fine, a very fine job."

"Not today," she said roughly, glaring at me a bit.

I accepted her feeling quietly, pausing again. "Laura, you know I was wrong in the way I spoke to you."

"Oh no," she returned quickly, in a whisper. "I was wrong. Ignorant, thinking the shop was mine—probably proving everything you've ever thought about Outsiders. Besides, how could you be wrong—you're the boss." Each of these words was uttered as if breaking free from a leash, yet whispered. The rage in her eyes as I looked into them filled my own heart.

"Now listen." My tone remained quiet as well, but I saw her hesitate at an intensity twice that of all my raving earlier. "I hardly need to mention that if you don't like it here—if you don't like me," I added pointedly, "you may stop coming here at any time. And no, I'm not such a weak willed, cowardly, self-ignorant old fart that I would take such a round-about way of telling you if that were *really* what *I* secretly wanted. If I ever decide I don't want you here, I will give you two weeks pay and tell you so—I will tell you the reasons why, to the best of my ability. And, Laura, I will trust that you won't show up with a gang of your terrorist friends and torch my place out of revenge. I trust you for that, do you understand?"

Her eyes narrowed, and I could see a tremendous eagerness fight, and falter, and win. "I wanted to do that today."

I held her eyes, and waited, no small amount of fear arising within me. I knew, though, that she absolutely had to speak next, and unprompted as well. At last, her eyes lowered for a few moments. When she looked up again there was a certainty there, some sort of Laura-styled peace. "But I decided I could never—would never do that. To—you."

"Why?" I asked, unable to keep the sigh of relief out of my voice.

To my surprise I saw a small smile on her lips as she took a sip. "I don't know. Some people—Outsiders" with a pointed look—"say I'm soft. On—Insiders."

"Well, do yourself a favor and think about it. Think about the possibility that maybe you want to try something different than revenge. Like...trust?"

Now she outright snickered, with a little shake of her head.

"I know, an alien concept," I teased her, delighted. "The

oppressed, battered Outsider trust the powerful, manipulative Insider? Soft in the head indeed. Laura, look at us. Look at us, you and me, really look!" She did, question in her eyes. "How much more power do I have over you than you have over me? Not figuratively, but literally? Tell me!"

She snorted in disbelief. "You could do anything you wanted to me—"

"Not could, would, dear. Of all the hideous things I could do to you, how many do you actually think I would do? Eh? Tell me!"

She thought, and shrugged.

"Just think about it. Imagine the me that you know, imagine of what you think I could really be capable. Now consider this: I'll tell you your power, a power apparently invisible to you, but not for long. You have an understanding of me and of what I hold dear. In a few minutes, in less than an hour, you and a group of your friends could destroy everything I hold dear, and me as well for that matter, and you know that leaving me alive would be the worse torture in that case. You know I take no precautions, have no security. Without you here, how would any Outsiders know the way I feel about my things? I'm relatively safe. but from now on, from now on, I am vulnerable to you." My throat caught, as I saw my words penetrate and swim around within her.

"But still—but still! If I ever decided I didn't want to or couldn't keep you on, I would let you go and not fear the consequences, because I trust you, I felt what you said before you said it. I didn't know for sure, but I felt it, and that is the essence of trust. Bearing in mind, of course, what I said earlier—-someone so intelligent, so fun, and so beautiful as yourself has nothing to fear. I like you Laura, as well. You must, you must trust me. You must speak your mind, like any normal human being, not cower and seethe like... like..."

"An Outsider?" but there was a trace, just a trace of teasing in her voice.

"Laura, you must try to forget all that while you're here. You must understand—some things." I paused, feeling uncomfortable. "I'm afraid I'm a typically spoiled Insider after all, in at least some respects. I try not to lash out at people when I'm feeling miserable, but I do anyway, at times. This isn't meant to excuse"

"Outsiders can be like that too," she actually interrupted me. The teasing had melted into kindness.

I smiled gratefully, moved and momentarily at a loss for words. "So. Anyway, I mean no harm, and you must simply speak up when I overstep myself. Do you know what I mean?"

She nodded.

"Also, I am accustomed to Marta dealing with customers, at least customers like Emma Unruh," I added with a wince. "I'm afraid I grew quite lazy in that area, and she was such a social butterfly—well now it's fitting that I step into that role more, at least until you are more accustomed to the way things are. And, I'm afraid it's kind of taxing, and what with it also reminding me of her death—well again, it's not by way of excuse—"

"I understand," she interrupted again.

"I'm glad," I said, sighing again. "It's just the only way we're going to be able to live with each other, day in and day out. Do you agree?"

She looked at me thoughtfully, then down once more. "I suppose."

"My dear, I don't expect you to merrily forget all the injustice done to you and your people overnight. Only this: to try and understand that your talents and qualities, and your desires for something different, something more, have brought you here, and my need for someone like you likewise, and to give yourself room to begin believing and trusting that, all right? And to see me as who I am, just a rather tired old man, really, because I can't, I won't bear the weight of all the atrocities of the world, all right?"

She did look fully at me. "Yes," she said quietly.

Our parting was easy, but it was long that night before the sight of her faded from my mind.

During the next interval of weeks, I realized with a sort of amazement the irony of myself, having made my life's small quantity of published work various articles asserting inherent goodwill and choice as the essence of human nature, being thrown into such close quarters with Laura, surely the world's most dedicated proponent of the antithesis of these concepts. Not completely, of course, or she would not have been there at all. And of course I had long hours of blackness myself, previously mentioned. Curiously, I noticed even amidst my wallowing at such times that we would quite flexibly switch roles: she would comfort and encourage me in a way that quite surprised me until I realized she did it more out of her affection for me than out of a change of beliefs. Her affection and also compassion. I realized that she identified with me all that she wished she could believe, so that when I failed or felt hurt, it was something she understood, although anxiety (if I turned increasingly bitter, what did that say for her hopes?) and self-satisfaction also mingled uneasily somewhere within her at such times.

Often I felt quite resentful of the entire situation. As she would have pointed out determinedly, of course I could have dispensed with her and almost instantly replaced her with someone of a sunnier disposition. Many delightfully unproductive hours were spent in contemplation of these possible replacements. Having grudgingly "given up my freedom" to marry after many long and quite immoderate years of complete sensual abandonment, only to find the intensity of pleasure multiplied rather than diminished with the focus of true intimacy, now I was left between worlds, and I was addressing the issue of how to resume my life with my usual indecision and endless inner debate.

I visited the gentler brothels. Their kind, skillful ministrations assuaged self-doubts and also some loneliness. But I had needed more than their comforts even before I had chosen to marry. I couldn't have been less interested in the sedate, practical sort of arrangement as would seem to be expected of me. My friends' ceremoniously casual introductions to their single female friends I tolerated only because I knew they were well-meant. Yet I was disturbed by more rambunctious desires and fantasies because they seemed to mock me and play into all sorts of very irritating stereotypes of what men my age are supposed to be going through.

So naturally the idea of a comfortable sexual relationship with a willing Outsider employee occurred to me. Such a thing, though, was commonplace to the point of mundaneity. Also, somehow the entire idea was vaguely disheartening, somewhat like becoming a brothel regular to the end of my days.

Many of the questions and alternatives I eventually found seemed to weave in and around Laura, in an indirect way. She was exciting: sheltered Insiders paled in comparison. True, she was younger than myself, but not young enough to make me feel foolish. There was a mental attraction, and a fundamental physical attraction that I knew was reciprocated. The final ingredient however was, albeit ultimately unnameable, something along the lines of an awareness, a pull that was at once subterranean and lofty, compelling and yet objective, spontaneous and yet, I felt, strictly and carefully controlled.

I was lost in the heat from her as she stood by me, shaken by a brushing wisp of hair. But what may appear to be repression or denial was nothing of the sort. The issue, the final and only one at this point in our friendship, was trust.

I watched Jack's face as she crossed the room toward us, a countenance so dear to me for so many years that every expression was transparent. His face opened to her with an appreciation that was only half exaggerated.

Looking at her, I saw she was fully aware of his attention, and that her cool, eyes-downcast Outsider act masked an immediate pleasurable reaction. After her usual, initial, penetrating evaluation via one brief glance at him, she focused completely on me. Only the very slightest, lingering lilt to each step, centered somewhere around the hips, gave evidence to reaction.

"Laura, this is Jack, a very, very, *very* old friend of mine."

"*Enchanté, mademoiselle,*" he said, kissing her hand. I watched her face emerge from its shell into an unrestrained smile of which I had never quite seen the equal, and as the fog of her hostility and fear lifted I saw a transformed Laura, looking directly into his eyes. Having witnessed this effect of Jack's many times over the years never diluted its charm and magic for me. As might be expected, however, in this case I felt some amount of annoyance and jealousy. Was that all she wanted, after all, a lot of flourishes? Some other, remote part of my mind independently murmured also, ah, so they're old friends too, but I wasn't really aware of this recognition immediately.

"You said she was beautiful, Paul," he said, keeping hold of her hand, "but there was one adjective, most appropriate, which you neglected to mention. Understandable," he glanced my way. Suddenly on his feet, he circled her slowly, elegantly transferring her hand from his left to right and back again. "And that word is...astonishing," he whispered into her ear.

Fascinated, I saw a heated mingling of expressions pass over her face as if through a veil of sea water. Raising her eyes to his face, very close to hers now, she said quietly but distinctly, smiling, "You're very kind," with a subtle accent on the last word, reclaiming her hand as well and circling around him to stand beside me.

Pleased, Jack sank back into his chair. "And intelligent too, so I understand. Where have you worked before, madam?" accenting the last word on his part.

"I have worked many places," still smiling.

"And your lover, what does he think of your working for an old lecher like my old, old, old friend Paul here?"

"Oh Jack, for God's sake," I interrupted, but Laura replied quickly.

"If I had a lover, sir, he wouldn't need to worry about my self-defense."

Sparkling with enjoyment, Jack leaned back luxuriously, hands behind his head. "That could mean many things."

"There's only one meaning."

Now all of us were smiling. Laura flirting! With an edge, of course, but it was flirting.

"Ah yes, well," Jack continued, "lecher or not, Paul always preferred the dove to the hawk. Birds of a feather, you know."

"Is that so? Then you're lucky, sir, for your kind would not require you to buy them the finer things in life...pearls, for example."

Jack looked at me blankly. "The Bible, Jack," I said. When he still didn't understand, "You know, pearls before..." gesturing.

"Ah, yes," he beamed, his attention returning immediately to Laura, the delight holding something darker now. "This may be true, but you'd be amazed at how many birds can be made to squeal."

"Yes, you would know that, wouldn't you."

"Oh, come now, let's not get ridiculous," I interjected.

"Oh, ridiculous isn't the word I'd use," Jack said. "It has been a pleasure, madam."

"Likewise," she replied. I couldn't see her face but I felt a guarded pleasure still in her voice. I wondered if all this was her natural reaction to Jack or (I admit the vanity of this) the result of a growing trust of me.

She asked me a question, presumably the reason she had come downstairs originally, and went back up.

"You're a coward, Paul."

"Oh, says you."

"I'm serious, you son-of-a-bitch, she's willing, and she wants you too."

Jack's eyes were as black and penetrating as Laura's when he was stirred. "Jack my friend, you are perceptive, I'll grant you that. But you don't know all that's passed between her and me in the past two months. You just have no idea."

"Oh, I believe you." He paused. "So you do want her then, don't you?"

"Well of course, in that way," I said uncomfortably. "I just don't know if—" and I struggled for words.

"Yeah, you don't know if," he said quietly. Scorn and envy seemed to be thoughtfully debating in his mind. "Well let me know if you decide nay and I'll repay you, my friend, and you won't be disappointed."

"Why wait?" I snapped. "Ask her now. It doesn't matter to me."

"Like hell it doesn't," he grinned.

"Jack let me try to explain it to you. I don't want what you want from her. Well—I do want what you want, but more. If she's willing to settle for the likes of you, well I'd rather know now."

"Ah, you torment her."

"As if she doesn't me!"

We looked at each other a few moments, things passing back and forth between us of which I was only half aware.

"Paul, I've told you a thousand times, a girl like that will not come to you if she hasn't already. She must be seized."

"Then seize her and shut up, for God's sake!"

Another minute passed.

"Call her," he said.

"You call her."

"Paul, call her downstairs."

"Laura!" I was tempted to begin fiddling with some stuff on my desk, but managed to refrain.

She came down the stairs and to me, not honoring Jack with a glance.

"My dear, Jack would like to ask you something. I don't know exactly what it is but I have an idea. Please handle him and the entire situation completely as you please, but above all, don't hold me responsible."

She looked at him coolly. It was as if the entire previous

interaction had not occurred.

Slowly, weightily, he removed his purse from his belt. His face cool as well, he removed his eyes from Laura only long enough to count out some bills, fold them, and place them on my desk.

"A month's salary. For one night."

Laura and I looked at the money, while Jack looked at her. She said nothing, and although I didn't wish to look into her face, I felt it was expressionless as well. Several long moments passed, and the tension began making me feel quite disagreeable.

Jack, on the other hand, seemed slightly encouraged.

"I mean no insult, my fine lady, and I hope the quantity I extend offers some proof of that. I may be a swine, but I am a direct and generous swine, and you have your friend Paul to vouch that you will not be harmed."

More time passed. At last she spoke.

"As I said before, sir, you're very kind. But...I've tried this kind of thing before and...I'm afraid I wasn't very satisfactory. I'd rather...not...try it again, although I am very flattered. Thank you," ...she began walking away.

Jack's eyes followed her, his face still expressionless. It was an artful reply and I thought I'd hear his familiar lustful sigh as he brushed her off with some remark, but instead I saw a red flush mottle his cheeks.

"I wouldn't wait forever for your friend sitting behind the big desk here," he said to her back. "His wife was killed by an Outsider, you know, so he's not likely to fulfill your little Cinderella dreams, no matter how much you might think he likes you."

I covered my eyes. I heard her steps falter and stop. "Jack," I said with no authority whatever left in my voice.

"Oh, you didn't tell her? Liberal to the bitter end, that's my friend Paul. Yes, my sweet, murdered in cold blood, by a petty thief. Could be someone you know. One of your friends, possibly, from the looks of you."

"Jack."

"Oh, all right, I'm going," he said, rising irritably. "But I'm leaving the money." I looked up as he reached her. She was looking at me, her eyes stark in the alien pallor of her face.

"I'll come round tomorrow. If you two find you're tired of mooning and masturbating over each other..." Suddenly he reached up and touched her cheek with the gracefulness possessed by some big men. She dropped her eyes from mine then, but did not look at him, and slowly turned away toward the stairs.

He watched her go, and then left.

For the remaining couple of hours until closing, I sat dispiritedly and did nothing. Fortunately no one came by. My thoughts were incoherent, my feelings sour. I heard no slightest sound from upstairs.

Finally I trudged up, no closer than before to knowing what, if anything, to do.

The room where she had been working was empty. I glanced out and saw the washroom door closed, so I walked into the studio to wait for her. I saw the pile of work on which she had started that morning virtually untouched, and smiled. Then I saw where she had spent most of the day, curled up reading a fine old tome. The chair and the book beside it reminded me of a painting, and I could almost see the outline of her on the cushion. My throat knotted: she was so dear to me, and I felt things would change soon, whether we liked it or not, and I had no control over how they would change. Looking aimlessly around, I happened on a few sheaves of paper sitting where some dim setting sunlight fell on them. Something unusual about them drew me closer.

My flesh chilled as I saw what they were. Laura had told me she drew but had never shown me any work. On the paper before me, surrounded by several crumpled apparent first drafts, was one of the most extraordinary figures I'd ever seen. The emotional impact cannot be articulated, but it was as if a male and female figure had been fused, yet remaining distinct. It was coitus, and yet it was also mother comforting son, and father nurturing daughter. Each way the eye saw seemed to flow into its opposite, or an alternate. Long before I had begun to finish looking, I heard her returning, and quickly moved to another place, for the drawing had the look of privacy.

We murmured greetings as if we were strangers, then I apologized for Jack, feeling overwhelmed with inanity.

She shrugged cautiously. "Why didn't you tell me...about Marta?" she asked softly after a few moments.

"I don't know," I said. "I wish I could tell you the reason, but I just don't know."

Some silence.'

"I'm sorry. About..." she said.

Like walking into shade, I felt a sadness emanate from her.

Upon entering the room she had walked immediately to her drawing and concealed it casually, as if straightening a picture. Now she lingered there; and I felt a desire to simply touch her that was so overpowering that my hand seemed to actually ache. I couldn't understand why I was filled with such futility, when I felt so strongly that she needed and wanted such a thing very much on her part.

Instead I felt myself reach for, yearn for some kind of truthful utterance. "I guess I thought I was trying to protect you," I sighed, "when I was really just...afraid of looking at how I really feel...I guess about Outsiders. Afraid as to whether..." I trailed off.

"I guess you think it would be a mistake for me to go with him..." she began, after some more silence.

"He wouldn't harm you, you know." She looked at me, and then we looked away, into another, strong, silent wave of moments.

"I guess it doesn't really matter anyway," she muttered with such a dark finality that I felt quite desperate.

"But it does," I blurted, "only—not as much to me, more to you. Do you see what I mean?"

She stood motionless. She reminded me of the suicide

49

taking one last drink, giving the world one last try through the lips of a bartender or other passing stranger.

"If it would be fun for you—I mean, you do like him..."
Neither of us could decide if this was a question.

"But...if there are other feelings...that you don't like, if it hurts you—don't do it to punish yourself. Or...me."

Her eyes covered my face then, and dove in through my own eyes, searching with such desperation that I felt like a pack of hounds had burst into my soul, only they had been running wild and so instead of baying they did their searching in a hunger-maddened, soundless frenzy.

After an excruciating few moments of this, she said, "You forget the money, too."

"Yes, I guess that would be all too easy for me to forget." I felt a ludicrous urge to offer her twice the amount, but even in my fog I knew this was so far off the point that the idea of it was stillborn. "It's there, if you want it," I said, suddenly, completely, finished. I turned away, and soon I heard her leave.

I saw the pile of bills sitting on my desk when I went downstairs, and I was filled with wonder.

The following day there was an unpleasantness with an ignorant special officer. Laura had seemed cheerful enough and Jack had fully recovered his usual menacing good humor when he stopped in. But there were residues of tension and frustration from the day before, and from troubling dreams both she and I had experienced that night.

I seemed to come conscious during a dream in a flash of emotion: it was from another time, with flowing white clothing, probably classical. I sat in a dim room, and others lounged around, watching. The air was heavy with indulgence, with corruption, for the scene was one of debauchery. Her knees on my thighs, her nude body trembling and sweating, a very young girl was before me. The most vivid image, one that haunted me for days, was that of my hand partly thrust into her, manipulating her in some way that I realized after waking I had fixed on as particularly, perversely pleasurable for me. Her clear fluids ran glittering down my wrist and forearm, first warm, then cold. Her hands tied behind her, she wept and occasionally struggled, but I was aware that this was no simple rape, that a bond existed between us, that there was some amount of consent and affection, but I was so overcome with a frenzy of lust, so utterly dissolute, so terrified of the years steadily carrying me toward my own death and the loss of all my wealth and power, that I was crushing this blossom in the very might of my embrace. I muttered, cajoled, and commanded in a constant flow, my overriding goal to force an orgasm from her, vindicating myself fully in my mind. Finally I looked up into her streaked face, and she looked down at me, and I saw the eyes of my own Laura. At that moment I began the separation, atom from non-atom, of myself from this other dream-self, into this existence, and my current self shrank from the spark of love swimming within the shock and terror in her eyes, a spark that was dampening, sinking, but not yet extinguished. I shrank in horror from the depths within the soul of that other me, of despair, obsession, and self-loathing, and the strength with which my own urge to love strained against the horrible, twisted constrictions I had bound around it in the ignorance and fear of that other time.

So it was with a mixture of relief and depression that I viewed my previous restraint of my desire for her that next day. My eyes, which had grown accustomed to surreptitiously trailing over her form from time to time during the months she had been with me, shunned her. I felt a detachment, almost a completion.

Nevertheless, the residue of feelings apparently attracted the official quite magnetically. It was a natural, if regrettable, predator/prey relationship between Laura and him. He made some ignorant comment, she smirked, and the hunt was on. In my debilitated condition I watched helplessly for some time before finally rousing myself to action. With her out of the room he was quite easy to handle, to flatter and plead that he have mercy on my "plaything."

This incident touched something quite deep within Laura. All the rage that continually simmered just below the surface of those black eyes burst free. There came a moment of decision for her, though, in which she could have fastened onto me to alleviate the force, the pressure of that rage. But, in a striking reflection of my moment of a quite different kind of restraint of the day before, she cast aside her weapon and, balancing on the precipice, she allowed me to lead her to our velvet room.

I spoke to her of her responsibility for her participation in the events that seemed to persecute her, through her belief in her own victimization, her fear, her rage, and her ultimate feeling of base unworthiness. Unable to think with any clarity whatsoever when I was looking at her, I spoke facing the window, and my eyes fell on some rather bedraggled rose bushes outside. On and on I rambled, and somehow some of what I felt for her was conveyed, some of what I hoped were more useful and true beliefs were interwoven in some kind of rose analogy.

She approached me, and finally there was a moment of transcendence of our miseries and preoccupations. My words, my feelings had touched her and although by no means convinced, she seemed to at least be willing to size up this new possible exit point for her anger, to mull it over, and that automatically altered it, relieved it of its deadly intensity.

She offered her gratitude. She offered herself as well, but in the framework of that gratitude. With my hand still tingling from the warm, slow dream-sheen of *her* other self's betrayed affection, I had no trouble in doing what was necessary: squeezing her hand and absolving her of any obligation. With my release of her, somewhere a book closed.

What followed that night was one of the experiences that encourage us to slog through all the other experiences through which we seem to have to wander to reach them. Jack bought me dinner, and on the way home whom did I see but my own dark rose, unexpectedly sprouting from her bus stop at that late hour.

I picked her up and offered to let her accompany me to my destination, the Baths, and quite easily accepted her demurral. By the time we reached her destination I was floating on some sort of inner river of events, and I could calmly watch her thinking, struggling with those final objections, while still feeling open to her, still feeling desire, still feeling love.

She came with me.

Then she came home.

Three

Ihad been sure when we climbed into bed that first night that I could not sleep. The glow I had felt, like I was a warm peacock gliding on air, when Paul and I had finally stepped up from the baths to dry and dress, had gone. The beautiful sleeping lawns and houses of his neighborhood seemed just as distant as ever to me, even though I was right there amongst them, and by invitation.

I had imagined Paul and me together before that night. Had dreamed, before ever meeting him, as many Outsider women do, of a wonderful, kind Insider rescuing me and taking me to his home. In these dreams, when I had managed to get around all the many obstacles between us, there was always a wonderful, final resolution that changed me: chased away all my fears and old habits of fear, placed me right at the center of his life, where I would be automatically safe and happy as long as he lived.

I was finding out very quickly that this was not to be so. By the time I stepped out of his car, the long minutes we had spent slowly, slowly touching, slowly feeling more, then wandering timelessly through sensations and emotions, arriving at a terror on my part that he felt and knew as he knew everything about me then, that he held and pulled until I felt it as a need, and then accepted—I wondered as I felt the cold night air how I could have thought of that as a kind of knowing. "There's always some of that in sex," the night said. "I am the only reality you will always truly know to be there."

It seemed so. I still didn't know how to touch him, what to say, and I knew he was unsure himself. No amount of mooning and grasping would have made it better, so I was relieved we were so quiet, in a way. It's frightening when a lover changes dramatically after that first time, either uncovering true coarseness of spirit or putting up new barriers, a beaver with a breached dam to mend. It was more frightening the times I found myself doing exactly the same thing, overcome by disgust, futility, or, worst of all, apathy. As far from my dreams of a life after rescue as it was, at least we were still just the Laura and Paul that I knew, what little I knew of us both, it seemed then.

I did sleep for a short while, deeply. When I awoke there was a wonderful stillness in the moonlight, and I felt that I was truly fully conscious for the first time in days. I looked at the face of my lover, the fine lines and etchings of time, felt and smelled his soft breath so close. I kept expecting his eye to open, catching me, catching me! But no, he was really asleep.

I got up and put on the robe he had lent me, aware of the strangeness of everything in the room. Everything except for my tired black dress, draped on a chair, an unwelcome familiarity. The room closed in then and I felt an inner draining away. The idea of belonging here seemed preposterous, almost dangerously so.

I wandered out into a living area, and looked at some of the lovely things he had there, only half seeing them in the dim light and with only some calm part of my mind really paying attention. That part oddly took everything for granted, but I was too unhappy to notice that then.

There was a big nook with cushions by a window, where the moonlight really streamed in. I picked up a book of medieval lithographs and sat down there, and stared out the window into a beautiful haunted back garden. I hugged my knees and sighed, annoyed to feel tears again after crying so much already that night.

After my mind had wandered for a while, Paul came into the room, and came to me and touched my hair and face. I looked at him, and he was sleepy, but, yes, his eyes were the same Paul. All in our loose white clothes, we looked like ghosts to me suddenly, kind of lost and out of place. I looked at him again, and this time I resisted the persistent fear that always made me look away. I held his eyes and felt cords unwinding inside me, and something very hot pushing up from my deepest core. This was the terror I'd been trying to avoid, an overpowering emotion that was also a physical sensation, an awful feeling of losing all self control. I finally looked away, stunned by the enormity of my fear. How could I be so afraid now when I had just been so close to him hours ago?

"Feeling a bit out of place, I'll bet, aren't you?" he asked, his hand still near me, touching me so delicately. I took it and kissed it, then drew my knees up and looked back out the window. I tried to speak a couple to times, shaking my head.

"I'll never belong here," I finally said as he nudged me aside and sat down.

"Time will take care of that," he said, his fingers still softly, slowly tracing over my skin, working a spell. That hotness inside again, some kind of womb-desire that aroused me but that mostly centered in my heart, my throat, my face.

"Maybe—maybe—you know, if you want to keep,—separate lives, and just see each other at the shop, I would understand. That would be okay, you kn—"

"You'd rather not come back?"

"No, I didn't mean that..." I had to smile, just a little. "I mean I understand that...with Marta having just died, I don't expect you to...you know—"

"Ah, you're not too sure of my judgment at this point."

"No, it's not that, really...I just wanted you to know I understand if you..."

"If I woke up tomorrow or in a week or month and thought, 'My God, what have I done? Who is this *Outsider* I've brought into my life, my home, my bed for God's sake? Sure, the sex was great, but how can I get rid of her now? God forbid, I think she actually thinks I'm serious about her.' Something like that?"

I laughed a little but some tears squeezed out too. "I just want you to know I wouldn't mind if you decided not to be lovers or only sometimes, or I can just work for you, as long as—as long as I don't—"

"Lose me altogether, eh?"

The hotness exploded in me and I leaned back into his arms and let myself want him so much, want this house, the new life I had begun to picture full-blown in my mind, painting and cooking and loving him every day.

"I love you Laura, you know."

"Yes, I know you said that last night, but that was—"

"I'm saying it now," and he turned my face to look at him. "I've been considering this for some time, you know, and I'm very sure of myself."

"I love you too," I said after a moment, watching him carefully.

He smiled slowly. "I'm very glad to hear that."

I looked back out the window, leaning forward again. "Why? Why me?"

"I thought I tried to say a little something about that yesterday."

"Yes, and I understand—and it was very—moving to me. But that's sort of why you *like* me, you know? I mean, why, with all the beautiful, wonderful women, Insider women—"

"To that, I'm afraid I don't have the answer any more than you," he said, sighing. "But really, why does anyone love anyone? Would we have loved each other under different circumstances?"

"You mean, if you were an Outsider?"

"Yes. What would you think of me then? Just a tired, old, rather ineffectual man, maybe working away unhappily at some menial job, maybe just sitting around all day, who knows, maybe even as bitter as you..."

We smiled and he winked at me. "I don't know," I said, studying him as if I could figure it out that way. "Sometimes I think it's not so much just that..."

"Oh really?" and I could see he had already thought about that too.

I looked away again. "I don't know—even if we had no differences, or obstacles, I've always stood on my own, you know?"

"Yes."

"And with you, even if we were hiding under a bridge somewhere in the rain, outlaws, you know? and just trying to survive, equals, maybe with me even taking care of you, in a way—"

"Yes?"

"Even then, when I curled up next to you to sleep, I think I would still feel like you were..." and I filled up again, "taking care of me, you know?"

"Yes, that sounds just awful."

"But it is, isn't it? I mean, why do I feel so..." He didn't help me now, I felt him waiting, so I tried to get through the fog to what I was trying to say. "You know I always stood on my own, I never felt I missed or needed a—a—"

"Provider? Protector? Father?"

"Right. I mean, I don't know about over here, but Outside a father could be a terrible burden as easily as a—a father. I never understood why women wanted someone to take care of them because—most of the time it didn't work anyway— they'd get thrown over because he would want a new younger model, or—or—die..." I looked at him, new awareness coming gently over me. This time the darkness in his eyes wasn't so frightening.

He touched my face again. "Despite all the degradations

of the marketplace in this age, the old father-daughter thing is still a problem, isn't it?"

"In a way, it has nothing to do with us, personally, you know? But in a way…"

"I believe that any taboo so strong is instituted to counteract a natural desire equally as strong."

I thought a few moments. "So you think the taboo's unnatural, not the desire?"

"More or less, yes. You know, my dear, putting aside all the people who've ever lived and all the misuses older men and younger women—or rich men and poor women, or people the same age or sex or class, for that matter, eh?—have inflicted on each other through time, and what our friends may say…" he winked at me again, because I was smiling, "and our age difference, and our cultural differences, and all our other differences, etcetera, etcetera, and what could be and what might have been, and knowing we need to each—each—keep standing on our own feet. Bearing all that in mind—do you think it's possible that if I stumble, you might be there to help me as you would help your best friend or your real father, for that matter, without wondering if I was unhealthily using and depending on you?"

I was shocked to see tears in his eyes, faintly, and hear them in his voice. I touched his face then, feeling like someone I had been joking with for hours had suddenly lifted his hand from his chest to show a gaping wound. I started to comfort him but he motioned that he wanted to go on.

"So do you think I would resent your weight if you were to stop straining forward and just lean back," pulling my shoulders gently toward him, "Rest your weight on me a little, now how's that, so very bad?"

Only when I relaxed and really lay against him did I realize how tired I was of resisting, and how very wonderful it felt to rest all my weight against a body that felt as strong as the sea.

I sighed and shifted to a slightly more blissful position. "I guess not," I said into a Paul-smelling neck.

My book of lithographs fell to the floor. "What's this?" he asked, retrieving it.

"There's some very beautiful stuff in there," I said. We idly leafed through. "We can be like them," and I pointed to a picture I had been reading about. A devilish-looking man in some sort of mask peered out of a window in a caravan-type structure. A devil's tail, presumably his, waved out another window. An equally licentious-looking woman, much younger, looked coquettishly out yet another. "It seems this fellow, some sort of warlock, seduced this religious girl, practically a nun, and carried her away, and they traveled around the countryside entrancing people and stuff."

"Ah, up to no good, of course..."

"Yeah, I guess she was practically a saint before he got to her..." I smirked.

"Oh I'm sure, poor thing, it's obviously this evil fellow's doing entirely. Obviously, he's bewitched her, for her to look so devilishly happy..."

"Yeah, I guess she does, doesn't she," I said, looking again at her profile facing her lover, and the little smile on her face. I read aloud the quote beneath the lithograph: "Were e'er a couple so wickedly free, as John of Blue and his sweet Cathy?" I found myself smiling, too, despite everything, and I ran my thumb over Paul's nipple and felt it harden.

"At least I don't have to feel guilty about corrupting *you*," he said into my hair, the same smile in his voice. My womb warmed me again and the book fell to the floor again, and the sun began to rise again, and we made love again, and nothing was over and everything was begun, once more.

Four

Icannot clearly bring to mind the first time that I beheld
John the Blue. I was quite young, and that event must
therefore remain lost forever in the mists of my girlhood.
With certainty I know that he passed through the pastures
and villages forming my childhood home some twice or
thrice the year. Such frequency was warranted then, of
course, it being before the coming of the present plagues,
with many more souls living on the face of the land than do
today. This provided much custom for a seller of ribbons and
needles, draughts and salves, such as John. Indeed, it was in
such an innocent role that he customarily appeared to most
all the folk, far from the fire-breathing, tail-lashing, pig-
footed demon leapt straight from Earth's hellish bowels as he
is now so oft depicted.

Clearly now I see the innocence of his role, but when I was
a child it was not so apparent. Part of the reason for this will
be obvious to anyone who knows children, or who remembers their own child years; that time before the dull and
angry veil of adult ignorance is lowered over the eyes (a veil

disguised as learning or common sense, whichever is most expedient), and the world grays and becomes so deathly ordinary. Children see mystery where adults see merely the decrepit; they see the average as quite rare, and the most commonplace events as new. This is to say, *any* peddler would have been a matter of interest; but John...to my quick imagination and sharp little eye, John Blue was a figure of magic.

By the time I neared my first year of womanhood, I had several facts marshaled to bolster this impression, which I pondered in secret, of course, having learned already through hard experience the necessity of discretion in speech. I had noted that news of John's approach made quite an impression upon certain of my neighbors and kin. The nature of this impression, I also noted, varied from one listener to the next. They, like I, appeared to feel a mixture of distaste and fascination in the anticipation of his appearance. But I did not quite understand why, as he had a hearty, jovial manner common to the peddler breed, along with a most ordinary enclosed conveyance, drawn by two most ordinary, middle-aged mares. And yet...was it only my excitable nature (a distasteful quality I was constantly assured would bring me to eventual ruin) which construed some shimmering aura of mystery about the man?

Full of dread that even my helpless fascination was some kind of secret sin, I hoped no one would notice how I craned my neck and stilled my motions, listening, whenever his name was mentioned.

As I have said, I saw my neighbors' reactions were peculiarly mixed. Among some, particularly the more pious members of our small local populace, there hung a vague air of distaste about his name as it passed from their lips. However, I was interested to note that this did not prevent them from eagerly seeking him out and purchasing his goods. Among others, there seemed a more dubious, alternating quality of comment, which perched uneasily on a fence of approval. Most bewildering of all to me was the wholehearted excitement I perceived in the flushed cheeks and Sunday frills of the young girls. Although I knew that such excitement is the rule among any group of females from here to Old China when offered the opportunity to buy rare and colorful ribbons and cloth, why did the wolf eat before hunting, I wondered, referring of course to the fine raiment worn merely to visit John the Blue.

"Why do 'Becca and Mary dress so fine only to see Old John?" I asked of my mother one day as we baked.

"They only wish to seem as nice as the things they buy," replied that pious worthy, scarce attending to me for the sake of the sod that would not light.

"But why do they wear only their browns to see Fat Jack, whose goods are equally fine?"

Only now seeming to construe the true slant of my inquiry, my mother exhibited there and then the very effect of which I have spoken, frowning with some heat and shifting her eyes. "Because they are foolish girls who shall be stricken by God if they are not careful, and you had best quit your idle wondering and attend to the beans as you were told."

Such distance into this mystery was all I ever accomplished, prior to my maidenhood, that is. This, however, in no way diminished but rather, if truth be known, increased my shared and private excitement and wonder in the anticipation of his arrival. My mind, prone to extremes as it was, ceaselessly whittled at each side of one question only: was he good or was he evil? For I was thoroughly convinced through all the teachings of the kindly Father Patrus and, later, the holy sisters at St. Mary's, that every creature on the Earth did clearly and irrevocably fall under the rubric of one of the other, if the truth only be seen clearly enough. Yet such contradiction about John presented itself that resolution seemed hopeless. Seemingly uncleansed by the sacrament, he yet found as much custom and favor amongst the pious, even the clergy, as among the profane. He sold wares and potions, probably unblessed, of unknown and most likely heathen origin from either the black, godless forests with their bewitched residents which surround our towns and farms, or countries placing many and sundry devils on high in damned worship; still those remedies performed their tasks as well as or better than those rendered by the churchly barber and midwife. He spoke shamelessly to the gaggles of girls and women, and manfully to the men, yet no foul rumor reached my ears of untoward assault nor seduction.

As for my personal acquaintance with the man, this was largely confined to stolen glances over the heads of my younger siblings on a visit to his caravan, or through a festival crowd. 'Twas a cause of some bitterness to me afterward that for all the preparation, the anticipation, for all the craning of my neck to catch the first glimpse of his caravan or his flaming red hair, I would be so overcome with a great timidity when at last in his presence that I would fall to scolding my charges, and engage in much intensive scrutiny of my sleeve (torn, was it? or not?) or the pattern of trees surrounding the caravan, or some lump of fair-spice just purchased. In short, I looked in any direction possible save toward the mocking, piercing eyes of John the Blue.

I have one clear memory of an exchange between us taking place just prior to the calamity, which, unbeknownst to our tiny hamlet was sweeping over all our vast land even then. Shooing before me my younger brother and sister, I approached his caravan on that day with my usual feigned indifference, but with throat-pulse pounding.

"Ah, 'tis our tiny Lady of Middlelea, with her two fine goslings, come to honor us with a call," he said, sitting in front of his caravan to have a pipe-smoke.

With my bosom just beginning to press the front of my dress, this much-accustomed comment (for so he had always addressed me) now caused betrayal of my studied coolness with a hot red flush. My thoughts jammed behind my tongue, all the clever retorts and saucy repartee seemed to wither on the vine, and I said nothing.

"Two new arrivals this year, I see," he continued, and I looked at him boldly enough then, for this was rubbish, was it not?

"You've gone daft at last, John Blue; these are Robbie and Bella, the same as I bring every year."

"Ah, don't try to play the innocent babe any longer, for the arrivals of which I speak belie that modesty—and you daren't claim ignorance of their pretty little heads bobbing along there just beneath your pretty throat."

I snorted with scorn then, and instinctively crossed my arms, then angrily placed them akimbo. "Two needles and two lengths of black thread, and stop your foul mouth, John of Blue."

"Come hither and stop it yourself, with your own or one of those pretty buds of yours," he said, grinning and not moving from his idle leaning.

"Tch, such a wastrel as yourself may find this hard to comprehend, but some folk hereabouts must work hard, and these include me, and I must be going, so do you want my penny or not? I ask you to decide very quickly so I may be on my way."

Well, long and hard did he laugh at me then, all the while with me standing there in a fit of pique. Robbie merely sucked his fingers, but Bella suddenly darted forth with a giggle, to touch his knee before I knew how to react.

"Ah, Bella!" he shouted out as if in great surprise. She reached for his hair and otherwise engaged in all manner of prankful endearments, to which he rejoined instantly in the manner of all those who are beloved of children. 'Twas only late that sleepless night that I knew the true cause of my misery at that moment: that with my own child years just behind me, the chance to sit carefree a while on the knee of John the Blue was forever lost, for I had never done so even at Bella's age.

"Bella come hither now or I shall beat you!" I cried.

John snatched her close then with another devilish laugh, "Nah, nah, Bella's coming with me, aren't you, my fair little girlie," to which she squealed in fullest delight and clung to his shirt.

"Aye, if she could breathe the fires of Hell itself, you would surely be the one to take her there."

"Oh, pay no mind to our stern Sister Catherine, my little sprite, we shall pay a visit to the little folk in Mersey's Wood. You'd come with me then, would you not?"

Bella shrieked and clapped her hands once more, and stammered somewhat of fairy princesses and the like.

"Very well then, keep her if you will and good riddance too, but I must be on my way. I shall stop around tomorrow once more," I said angrily, and turned on my heel and marched several steps away.

"Cat-tee!" cried Bella jumping down and running to me.

"Oh, lower your dainty nose a moment and I'll get your damned wares, you little nun," John growled, arising with great slowness.

"And mind your tongue around the child how you speak of St. Mary's! But for the nuns, folk would have run wild long ago what with the bad crops and the new tariffs, and you'd have no custom at all."

"Oh, so says you, and where did such a little slip of country girl find the mind to so comprehend the governance and movements of these here parts, eh, tell me that?" he said, entering his caravan and coming round to the little wares window.

"Sister Theresa has been so kind as to tell me all, thank you, and as she is able to read and write I would wager she knows more than the likes of you!"

"Oh, one cow telling another far from makes it true. Women's gossip it remains and always will so," squinting his eyes and curling his lips in an odd smile.

"They're not women they're—brides of Christ," I said, almost forgetting how to speak in my wrath. But truly, although I sputtered and pecked in my movements, as if in continuing anger, inwardly I marveled at how he always knew to touch my sorest heartwounds, for ceaselessly from everyone did I hear of my unnatural, prideful, headstrong ways and how they would bring me to naught or worse due to my place and sex.

"Aye, their juices dried long ago, but yours, your rivers have just begun their coursing, and soon enough your arms will be so full of Bellas and Robbies of your own you'll not spare one thought to higher matters over the course of a year," John said. And somehow through my pique, for a shadow of a moment only, it seemed, oddly, that he meant no insult to me directly—but in my haste for rebuttal my fevered mind passed over this glimpse, and I forged ahead.

"Not I," I muttered, pocketing the goods and turning to leave.

"Oh, and how do you plan to escape your fate, tell me that? Unless you mean to build a shack and hide in it like the loony widow Widge?"

I was suddenly loathe to reply, for we had now, with John Blue's typical unerring homing-pigeon course, neared the tenderest and most fragile of all my fevered hopes and dreams. Despite my reluctance, however, my blood remained too hot for me to quell my speech, and I turned suddenly to make defense. "Sister Theresa has promised that should I continue helping them and learning my catechism and acting in all ways obedient and chaste, that I may yet have a place there at St. Mary's."

Well, with that he let loose the roundest guffaws. "You could go so far's to take your vows and set your altar, but you know damned well should some moneyed city girl offer to buy her way in you'd be booted straightaway out the back door, for your holy friends have eyes that light for money just like the lowest heathens. And you know damned well it's true!" he ended with a sudden dreadful intensity.

"She does not lie to me!" I whispered hotly, but his eyes were hurting me still.

Then he looked oddly at me for some long moments. "That may be true, my little nun, but it matters not a whit, and you know why, don't you?" With his look so full of meaning, some dawning, awful awareness began to stir behind my mind's sight. "Come inside this place with me next springtime and I'll show you what you're made of, if half the louts for ten miles around haven't done so already," he said in such low menacing tones that fear of I hardly knew what leapt within me. Furious at my helplessness, but helpless nonetheless, I stood staring at him. "Aye, your beloved Sister Theresa shall be seeing your true nature soon enough, and when she does come you round and see old John the Blue. Sit you on my lap a while and you'll marvel at ever dreaming you'd keep those tender thighs closed for all eternity, my sweet."

I turned then, saying nothing, and wept all the way home, although my mother under her burdens noticed not a thing. My mind, which once I prized as clever, seemed to be drowning in the rush of all the feelings conjured by his words.

The winter following was exceptionally strong. Harvest was meager and the lord who claimed to protect us only exacted yet more tribute from what little we reaped, while protecting us not a whit from the plunder of robbers and soldiers of neighboring lands. Also, nightmarish tidings from near and far began to reach our ears, of a dreadful plague of sores and death the likes of which had never been seen in living memory. Where once our folk had been hospitable enough as far as our means allowed, now strangers were hard pressed to find an open door. So great was the toll of suffering and death that the more pious among us wailed the doomsday chant with increasing fervor: we must be damned indeed. Truly, although deprivation had been my lot all of my life, that winter seemed even to my young perception to likely be our death or at least my own.

The sisters at St. Mary's suffered with us, and yet what a refuge the quiet stillness, the clean floors and clothing, and the ordered, kindly faces of the abbey seemed to me in contrast to the horrors of the outside world. My father's back was breaking under labor three times the quantity that would allow proper rest; often he came home merely to collapse and not move for the few hours of respite allotted him. I questioned and beseeched the Virgin, to what end? To sustain my mother and sister and myself (Robbie died that winter) merely so that we may grow to do the same? I longed for the greater purpose contained within the walls of the convent. Hunger and cold and fear there were, and yet the prayer, the beauty of the surroundings, and the ceaseless, foremost dedication to God and duty dulled the pangs. All this I felt in the short times I spent there: What inconceivable reward, I wondered, must accrue to actually dwelling within its walls?

Through that long winter my high regard and affection for Sister Theresa grew also. Some ten years my senior, she seemed the embodiment of all virtue and beauty of which flawed womankind seemed capable. In truth, much time did I spend, whilst scrubbing or mending, searching my mind for this womanly flaw, for all holy teaching and common wisdom alike placed woman at the heart of all mankind's trials and tribulations. Yet, such was her diligence, her virtue, her kindness, so notably was she lacking in vanity, pettiness, lust, and weakness, that I was hard pressed to find the fatal flaw.

Indeed, in the way of young girls, steadily through that winter my devotion to her grew to exceed the bounds of common friendship and approached the realm of infatuation. I strove mightily to quench the womanly stirrings that so took me by surprise each time, that so dried and humbled the proud intellect I held privately so dear. Just as I was perplexed to see no flaw in my beloved when my teachings indicated I must, so at times did I guiltily, furtively ponder the nature of these feelings: by name must they fall under the huge and monstrous wing of the Demon Lust. And yet they felt very sweet, and seemed to harm no one. More so, the common lust evinced everywhere the eye alighted in our land was evil enough, but the unnameable lust elicited by the love for one's own sex—for such in truth I felt for Theresa by winter's end—was by nature so appalling that I refused my thoughts their habitual pursuit of any mystery. I inflicted severest restriction upon them, turning them to thoughts of God or, when this was to no avail, drowning them in penance and voluntary pain. Winter's cold being the readiest punisher available, I took to applying snow or ice to myself in my furtive efforts to quench the heatful ardor. Death from any resulting illness was to be preferred to its deadly allure.

As Fate or God would have it, though, there came one evening by start of Spring when my hopes were crowned and plunged within moments. Her sweet green eyes alight with some secret mystery, Sister Theresa pulled me into her little cell and, after taking my vow of silence, confided that she had spoken with the Mother and obtained an unofficial promise of my acceptance into the abbey as of the next Michaelmas. So great was my joy that I clasped her once and then again to my bosom, for she it was who had petitioned on my behalf. Suddenly I was flooded with a rushing tide of all the strong emotion and feeling I had struggled to uproot, and, hardly knowing how or why, I kissed her face and lips in teary gratitude and love, and with abandon. In truth she did not resist overmuch: I felt stirrings beneath my hands and mouth which betokened a return of my affection. This caused me to pull up short, not with a curbing of desire, but to see into her eyes as to the meaning of this. A haunted waiting I perceived there, and, all unknowing in my mind but, suddenly, not at all unknowing in my flesh, I drew my lips near hers again, for another kiss.

A tiny noise we heard then in the hall. Back we jumped at once as from the Garden Snake itself, and turned to see Sister Margarethe standing there. Vivid still remains my memory of an instant-born bitter remorse, which I saw reflected in the countenance of my beloved. 'Twas not the shape of Margarethe's expression that gave notice of her disapproval, but rather the arrows shot from her eyes, arrows as steely as a drawn sword. The force of God seemed embodied in His choice of witness, for none had taken such dislike to me as she, and none dwelling within those walls was so strict and grudging with joy of any kind. Therefore those narrowed eyes held, besides their immediate condemnation, a vindication of all evil she had seen in me before.

I fled the place without a word; my feet might have run on cushions of water for all I felt their weight upon the cold stone floors. Out I ran into darkness; Spring had begun to venture out by day but retreated yet by night, so 'twas Winter's breath I sucked. I stumbled blindly across the field and past the sleeping gardens into forest's cover, my mind stunned but sensing hurt so huge and overwhelming that it gladly seized on straining eyes and legs and feet to keep that hurt at bay.

Surely all was lost. (What can match the shock of sudden despair to the young and keen of heart—before there is wisdom from past survival of despair on which to draw? The giving way of pain to time seems inconceivable until known through strong experience.) I staggered onward for quite some time, gasps giving way to sobs and back again, unheeding of the mortal's chief responsibility when the unpathed forest first is pierced: to watch and track the place and way. Already had a shape begun to form in the back of my mind, its purpose to block that encroaching hurt for once and all, and this shape had no need for vigilance.

I passed through the trees for a full hour or more, until the pain of cold in my feet had almost numbed, and a peculiar calm enshrouded me. Now my mind seized on the huge beauty and silence all round about me. My life at the abbey began to seem quite long ago and far away. The frozen spirits reached out their twigs and leaves and roots to slap my face and bring me to my knees, seemed bent on capturing me, and yet did then uncaringly release me. Well I knew the peril to my immortal soul should they succeed, yet I was strangely uncaring.

Finally I came to River Moire's edge, shining most beautifully beneath the sliver of moon perched high above us. I sank down to a log nearby, uncaring of the dampness that must quickly seep through. For another full hour or more then I sat, weeping slowly and entering into a strange dialogue. I turned my heart and voice to the Virgin, for no saint possessed such vividness in my mind as She. Abjectly I laid my sins at her feet, my evil and tainted character, my stained hands and mouth. Then I lapsed into silence, and contemplated the horrors of Purgatory surely awaiting me should I execute that plan toward which my whole self seemed to yearn. A trembling with cold and fear began deep within me and moved out to my limbs as I weighed my few miserable alternatives. I doubted whether there were absolution for my crime, but even were there such, then only long and dreary years, possessed and used by some as yet unknown husband and grasping children, were all that lay in store. Yet, should I make the Moire my bed this night, 'twas possible I would spend all eternity burning most miserably in Hell: Purgatory did not release such a person ever, some felt, although Theresa had expressed belief otherwise when Henry Roberts had hanged himself.

Long did I plead with Her for a natural release from these earthly chains, for Her to simply squeeze my heart gently in Her blessed hands and remove this awful choice which lay before me. I would endure any horrors she deemed fit for many long years, I offered, if only, if only to be released at the end to serve with the other blessed hosts of heaven at her feet, forever more. And yet, I knew well that, God's laws being immutable, there should be no exception for a lowly, evil wench such as myself. I looked back on my life with new eyes, seeing many actions, desires and thoughts in a new, shadowy light, saw myself damned from the start, it seemed, and at the end, there remained nothing within me but a lasting darkness.

Finally, I rose to stand on the bank. I clutched my wrap more closely about me as I stared into the Moire, and the tiny part of my mind still able to do so wondered at my body's last tenacious grasp on its feeble warmth, on this, the brink of eternity. It seemed to me then that I had already half died with the cold, all my heat having passed through my eyes and nose into the snow.

Closing my eyes and fixing my mind, heart and very soul on my image of the Virgin, recommending myself into Her hands, I fell into the water. Agony made me gasp, but half of what I breathed was water which then became a sword that pierced me through and through. Very soon I felt no more.

Time stopped with sensation. Darkness replaced my pain. I felt a movement, a rushing forward, but only of my essence, as in my many dreams of flight. Steadily in my fear did my heart fasten on Her, never letting go, and after some unknown interval, I was rewarded with a sight of light that was at once Love. It grew and grew, and centered on a figure in white. It was She—and just as She appeared on the Abbey chapel wall! My heart full to bursting, I sought and found her eyes, and at that moment, when She beheld me, I was flooded with a Love beyond the heights of my dearest dreams. Smiling was She, and looking straight at me, and I knew Her and knew Her to know me, with all my most secret and public thoughts and acts, which seemed to somehow actually pass between us—down to that last moment by the river, when I was overcome with the most dreadful fear and regret, and I turned from Her, unable to witness disappointment in her blessed face, a disappointment worse than the harshest anger from any mortal. Instantly fires sprang round about me, as I knew they would, and for some time I felt their licking me round and about, and I endured them as I knew I must. Yet still I spoke to Her with my mind, blessing and thanking Her for those blessed few moments when I had been graced with Her presence. More deeply than before it seemed I felt my evil, and remorse, and despair, without the distractions of cold and choice as mitigation. This feeling grew and grew, and the fires burned hotter and hotter, until it seemed I could bear it no longer. Oh Virgin, I yearned, have mercy, have mercy, until it seemed the force of my desire would burst the bonds of my very soul.

And then...the fires were quenched, the darkness lifted. Once more I felt and then saw Her presence, and She smiled upon me once again. I looked down and saw myself to be in a green field, with blue sky and trees, fairer than the sweetest summer day of my mortal experience. Betwixt us was a river, which I knew to be the Styx, but yet we still saw and heard each the other thoroughly. And I knew, with more conviction than I knew my name or my mother's face, that God's mercy outweighs His judgment.

"Mother," I said to Her, and it seemed my heart wept with joy.

"Yes, my child," She said smiling, all full with Divine love.

"Is this place heaven?" I asked.

"Yes, it is."

"Then I am forgiven?"

"Yes indeed, my child, you need suffer no more."

"But—what of the fires, and the teachings of the priest, and my—sin?" I asked, bowing my head, and it seemed a shadow passed across the land.

"Your heart has shown you the truth, as do your eyes now, is this not true?" She asked gently.

Looking back up into those eyes, my heart blossomed once more, and I stepped closer to the river, where a kindly bearded man now waited on his skiff.

Suddenly there was a pulling and tugging, and I looked back over my shoulder to a shaded world I knew to be the Earth.

"Who is there?" I asked.

"'Tis someone who needs you," She said.

Somehow I knew it was not my mother or father, or Theresa, or anyone of my usual acquaintance, but someone else, someone dark and yet...and yet I sensed more of this person than my little soul could yet perceive. Slowly, with effort I turned back to face Her. The sight of Her filled me with yearning. "But I want to come to you!"

"As you help him, so shall you help yourself," She said

with the first, tiniest hint of sternness. Yet that speck seemed a vast ocean, so greatly did I yearn for Her full approval, and to give to and serve Her every need and desire—for eternity. I knew She hinted at that fatal final act, and thus was born another choice, just when I had thought myself beyond them.

"Do you understand?"

"Aye," I sighed, feeling that pull once more, this time acquiescing, with great reluctance, and yet acceptance, for I knew Her meaning fully.

As can be imagined, long and frequently since that fateful day have I dwelt upon its significance, for in truth I date all my life as either before or after its occurrence. How could a vision of the Virgin have so undermined the teachings of those purporting to be Her representatives, namely the priests and nuns sworn to her service? Never again after that meeting could I fully accept their threats of damnation as final truth. My only answer is that Her mercy and wise beauty placed me high on a strange plane, from which I viewed all my acquaintances and kin with a kindly and forbearing eye, yet also with this strange understanding of the flaws in their conception of the Truth. In short, I was jolted from the dark and dreary reverie my life had seemed until then, never to be quite restored. Yet withal, I was possessed of a great tenderness for all of them, and felt no rebellious urge nor wanderlust. In truth, the Abbey and all its servants seemed dearer than ever to me in their striving and their effort to be pure and good, and to uplift the grievous suffering of others.

Such then was my state of mind as I descended to the earthly plane again, shaken and confused, and yet sustained by the Light and Love I had seen above.

My first breath, on returning to this world, restored to my wandering spirit all the agonies of mortality with an ax-like blow. I coughed and retched uncontrollably, only faintly aware of someone's hands assisting and holding me. Finally my aching, tearing throat cleared just enough so I could breathe with ragged gasps. The darkness was full, the sliver of moon was gone, and the Moire still whispered beside me. I knew nothing of who it was who had quickened me and now lifted my body to bear me away, aside from his being a male whose strength matched his task. My burning eyes and weakness bore me back to the nether regions again, for how long I knew not.

When I awakened again, darkness lingered still—but the warmth! My body was intoxicated by the sweet, delicious warmth gently wrapped about it. The very air was warm and faintly scented, and a tiny room revealed its contours, limned in the red of hearth, not the white of moon. I saw the tiny brazier with its glowing coals first of all, and next some odd-shaped things, with bottles and books and more. I coughed again suddenly, turning to discharge some small residue of my recent watery sojourn onto the floor nearby. Just as quickly a hand appeared from the darkness beyond the coals to hold a bowl beneath my mouth, which I grasped with gratitude.

"Aim well and live again, child," growled a friendly-seeming voice nearby, a voice I recognized with shock as that of John Blue. I dashed the retching tears from my eyes, the better to behold him in the tiny light, and I saw the jut of beard answering red to the fire, and sparks of it in his flying hair as well. The next instant my shock deepened: this must be the infamous caravan in which he dwelt. And in it now I lay helpless and ill. I crossed myself immediately, as fear compounded fear and flooded my body, I hoped, with strength sufficient to fight or flee.

"I like that," he grumbled, rising. "The wench tosses her soul to Hell, and yet asks Christ's protection from the one who retrieves it for her."

Stunned, I merely watched him, and could think of no answer. Deftly he added something to another bowl on a tiny stove rack, sending steam into the air with a fizzy infusion of scent. Before I could react, he shifted to sit on my cot, and lifted my shoulders to drink. I did not fight, for such would have been useless. However, I shut my lips fast. I could muster at least some resistance at least to this potion.

"Come now, Cathy, this draught contains no harm or evil spell. 'Tis either this or out you go forthwith, to find your way home as best you can. I'll not harbor some sniveling, nun-ridden brat within these walls, thank you."

I looked at him then uncertainly, for in truth his tone was growling but kind, and seemed somehow innocent of deception. "What is it?" I asked.

"'Tis for your ague, nothing more," and he named several local roots and common ingredients.

Downcast as I was, and feeling within a burning chill and a spinning queasiness that made the thought of braving the night outside unendurable, I sipped the fizzing brew, at first reluctantly, then with an eagerness seemingly beyond my control. Its taste was bitter and not pleasant, yet my ravaged gut welcomed it nevertheless.

To follow this, he then encouraged me and reset my position with such comforting word and gentle motion that I wondered if in my delirium I mistook him, so different did he seem from the John Blue I knew before. In truth his quiet kindness overwhelmed me and put me in mind of She whose presence I had only just quit. This memory opened the door to a full, heavy memory of those events just recently passed. My heart filled with sadness unspeakable, yet, fearing his ridicule, I let no movement cross my face.

Something of a shadow he naturally saw, however, for he leaned back, and, resting a foot up, took my hand and held it firmly, all the while regarding me steadily. Slowly I raised my eyes to his: once arriving at their target, there they rested. What passed from eye to eye within that frame of time and place cannot be said while still adhering to those terms. Huge tears squeezed out of my eyes and crossed my cheeks to run into my hair; in my fever and child's mind it seemed he knew all that had happened, and all that I felt, without my telling him a word.

From that midnight until the following afternoon I passed in and out of sleep, and gathered the storm of sickness in my body. My soul in its delirium trod the paths between this world and the next without noting the common boundaries and posts marking their borders. Lucid moments of sensing the cup gently held to my mouth, of feeling myself alone for some time, of watching gray light slowly grow 'twixt the cracks in the window shade, of seeing John Blue's movements once again in our warm shell, alternated with wandering dreams and grating reiterations of the previous day's events along with bits of Abbey protocol and routine.

As the sun yellowed, I seemed to alight on Earth once again. I looked across the grate to see John Blue dozing in his bunk. Seemingly suspended above my aches in a frothy gauze of lightness, I dwelt some moments on the creases of his face and what they said to me.

Of course his eyes then opened, and the greenish spark which leapt from them to me twitched the corners of my mouth into a smile before I looked away.

"She lives again," he said with a smile to match mine, "and even shows a falling-off of favor toward the burden she had lovingly couched here now."

I smiled a little once more, and looked into those eyes again. Suddenly I felt no fear or reluctance to do so, and idly I wondered if this were a true spell, this loss of modesty and threat in the gaze of a strange man. Still I made no reply, for nothing in my experience or teachings provided protocol for such a situation. He knew much of me, body as well as soul, I knew from the bareness of my skin against the blankets and the emptiness of bladder and bowel I could feel within. And yet gross familiarity of speech might bring on the lechery and fearsome mystery I knew to be contained in him.

"Has the Moire kept your tongue, then?" he asked. "Next time I pass her banks, shall I hear it lecturing the fish on their sinful ways, to procreate without the blessing of the Pope?"

"Nay," I said with another smile, "'tis simply I know not what to say."

"Start then," he said, sitting again on my cot and handing me a cup of broth he'd had warming, "with unburdening yourself of what weight could pull you down so to such depths."

I sipped, and took spoon and ladled heavenly broth into my mouth. Meat and greens I tasted in there as well as potato.

"I am damned, is all there is to me," I sighed darkly.

He rested his foot up once more and, leaning back, sucked on his pipe. "What could such a tiny thing have done to earn such reprobation? Have you slit your mother's throat, then?"

"There are other manner of sin than those known by the likes of you, John Blue."

"'Twasn't me a-drowning not too long ago. 'Twas I who pulled you free, if I recall."

I caught his meaning and bowed my head to show it. "'Tis true, I doubt if even you have ever thought, less done, what I have done yester-eve." He sat quiet as before, but now with full attention on my face. Caught between distractions among my kin and neighbors all my life, 'twas an eerie feeling to be the focus of this full stillness of his. "Right you were last Fall, when you said that—" and tears pinched my voice a little "—that I were not fit for the nunnery."

"As I recall, there was no talk of fitness, only of suitability. The nightingale is not suitable to chew on, its purpose being altogether different."

I looked at him sharply, for I could not believe such sweet words were not said in jest. But he did not smile or leer, only gazed intently, full with meaning, into my eyes.

"You are kind, John Blue, although I know not why, and when I tell my sin, I dread—" and I choked on tears again.

"Try this old ear, child, and delay no more, for decisions must be made between us two before the day is done."

The thought of yet another choice before me was the final push, and out spilled my story from the Abbey, amidst my tears. "Now say what remedy there be for one so evil and unnatural as myself. I am not fit for mortal Christian marriage, much less marriage to Christ."

He took my hand then, and squeezed it warmly until I once more met his eyes, steeling myself for whatever he might say. "Cathy dear, I know what folk have to say of me, and moreover what they think, which beacons through their eyes and faces clearer than their words. But credit me with this: that with some forty years' walk upon this Earth, and with the distance of that walk extending to other lands of which you'll never hear, much less see, that I may have seen and heard of much you do not know. Is that within your ken?"

"Aye."

"And although the devil may hide within these walls somewhere if what some say is true, still, have I not also evinced some conduct independent of his sway? Will you give me that as well?" he asked sternly.

"Aye," I admitted.

"Then, lying and ignorance put aside for now, will you believe me when I say this 'sin' is, far from unknown and original with you, a common and lovely thing in other lands and circumstance?"

I looked up short in disbelief. "Aye," I snorted, "in heathen lands filled with low savagery no doubt, unblessed and damned as I am."

"Aye, if so you must phrase it, but I speak also of the folk within the walls of none other than your precious cloister, my sweet," he replied with some irritation.

I stared at him in open-mouthed wonder. "Lies, such—lies!" I sputtered, and yet...and yet I felt within my mind a clicking of doors from their locks, which heretofore had been shut fast. My inner eyes, despite myself, followed peering through as I looked away.

"Ah, yes, your churchly mind protests, and yet the one within you who knows as much as any man who ever lived knows that what I say is true, for does it not explain some heretofore mysterious things?" he murmured.

Sisters Agatha and Anne, Sister Caroline's wandering hand one day in gardening, young Pete from over the rise, odd hints and words in talk between others, many tiny events flitted across my mind's eye.

"Mark these words, child: if that be all that's brought you to this brink, you've naught to do but return to your cell, make full confession, and you shall be shriven as with any other sin."

Quietly we sat for some moments whilst I brooded on these words and watched my fingers folding and creasing the wool of his blanket.

So odd and new were the thoughts passing through my mind that I almost forget who it was gazing upon me so quietly. "Surely...Theresa..." I began with some incredulity, continuing to review inwardly the events of past years. I sought his eyes again, and, against my will their dancing forced a smile from my lips. "You don't mean to say that she...knows of such matters...and has never spoken of them to me all this time?"

With this he laughed with all delight and mockery. "One so stern and righteous as yourself does not invite such confidences, did that thought ever cross your mind?"

"That's not so!" I returned, feeling quite stung. "Many confide in me, Sister Theresa above them all! I know much about many goings-on all roundabout these parts!"

"And much passes you by on its rounds, perceiving in your interest and temperament a lack of welcome. You are known as, with some grudging respect, mind, one of those who actually believes it possible to live by the words of the priests."

" 'Tis possible, with much effort and all humility!" I returned hotly, much rankled now. " 'Twould be far easier without such as you who believe in nothing and make no effort at all!"

"You're sure of that now?" he said, with such a dark, seasoned amusement, that I felt quite young and foolish, and ceased my heat.

"It must be possible to live with one's face turned to the heavens instead of the dirt, to act rightly and not hurt others, to not be greedy or lustful or disobey the priests," I muttered stubbornly, my eyes downcast again.

"And your St. Theresa, she believes this as well, I suppose."

"She believes we ought—but that most shall not," I admitted darkly. "She does live so, as near as I can tell. Until..."

"Until you thrust your tongue between her lips and damned her eternally," he mocked.

I felt a queasy flush arise within me and spread across my face at that, and I turned my face away.

" 'Tis a sad sight for these old eyes to see an act of such innocence and love cause such pain, and to one of such beauty," he said.

I found his eyes again then with some wonder, at once my tears finding mine. I was becoming accustomed to him with uncanny rapidity, but I could not stop myself, so much better did he seem to know me than did my own mother. And, having seen no evidence of his meaning harm thus far, on the contrary...'Beauty'! " 'Tis the Devil's work, to tempt one into vanity..." I murmured, but with great unsteadiness.

"Aye, but the sin lies in the heart that would listen, is that not the way it goes?"

I touched my face then, and straightened my hair, all unaware of my actions until after performing them. Was this indeed not what was meant by a spell? For if anyone in my experience would be familiar with casting such, I was sure at that moment it would be John the Blue.

"If such careless words spoken by such a knave as I could cause your heart to bloom," he said, "think you on the effect of the full sunshine of your devotion on the petals of your Theresa's heart."

"There is proper churchly reply to all you say, John Blue, and it means nothing that such a week and foolish vessel as myself cannot make it at this time," I cried in all frustration.

"Aye, and what was her reply when you touched her with dread temptation?" he continued, regardless of my words.

I shook my head and snorted with much stir. "She would not approve—"

"I care not for approval, for it bends the truth unrecognizably. I ask you what she did," he said sharply, in a way that pushed my tongue to speak the truth alone.

"She...she..."

"What did you feel beneath your hands and mouth, and see within her eyes?" he pressed.

"I felt her move..." I cried at last, with tears now freely streaming. "She moved in my arms, and kissed me too, and in her eyes..." but I could not go on.

"Hold her eyes fast in your mind, child. The flesh speaks that truth which the tongue dare not."

"But—that is—blasphemy!" I shouted in sudden rage.

"Then your beloved is not so far above it as you believed, is she? And I am here to tell you that no mortal living is, and if that be your truth we are a damned lot indeed," he said in some heat, rising and busying himself. "Prepare yourself, I shall ride you home forthwith."

With these words I was unaccountably filled with dismay. I sat still a moment in all confusion whilst he moved about. "Nay," I said, finally.

He turned to look at me, seemingly in surprise. "Nay?"

"Nay. I will not return as yet."

"Why not?"

I searched for words. "I...cannot."

"Why not? You have the strength to sit astride my mare awhile."

I cast my eyes about with growing desperation, and with relief they fastened upon the coverlet. "This sacking is ripped clear up—I must stay to repair it—as betokens my gratitude," I said, letting some small part of my true meaning go forth from my eyes to his.

He appeared indecisive for a moment, but I kept my eyes on him, in supplication, if truth be told. "One night's survival in the cold your kin will believe," he said, "but not two, and I won't have them know you spent them here."

"Neither would I," I replied at once. "They shall not miss me: those at home shall believe me at the Abbey, and those at the Abbey shall think me home, and I shall not set them aright."

For once I welcomed his amusement. "Your words, begging your pardon, my fine St. Cathy, have a suspicious ring of deception about them." When I smiled, he continued, "When once embarked upon such a path, take you care to trace it well, lest you become as lost as you were yester-eve."

His words sobered me as I took the stick of meat and the crust he offered. What path indeed had I embarked upon? All I knew was that the thought of returning to my life just yet filled me with an unendurable weariness. Whereas here... and my eyes roved over all the mysterious and mundane objects which cluttered each area of the caravan. What would 'Becca and Clyde say if I related all that I saw?

"Mark you as well," he said with meaning, "I have trod those paths for many years, and if you have your mind set on deceiving me, you shall see and feel the 'Devil's work' firsthand and lose what name and place you have. Heed me now, Cathy, I am in all seriousness when I say that we shall not be known to have been together these nights, is that understood?"

I was quite abashed at this, for it seemed quite clear he had heard my thoughts as if spoken. "Aye, I swear it," I said quickly, and meant it, too.

I sewed a little on the coverlet, but soon my head dropped for further sleep; when I awoke, the needle was at my side. I took it up but John stirred again, and took it from me. He bade me sit up, and examined me all about, asking me questions, bade me cough, and so on. His hands were so gentle, their ways so mysterious, that I felt quite overcome, and could not meet his eyes.

"The morning then," he said with a sigh as he rose, and I saw that he was weary. "You shall be fit." Then we lapsed into silence for a while, except for those few words necessary for the small tasks of the evening.

The fever and chills and various other pains had largely passed, as well as the larger doubts about my coming future. In their place, however, my dreams had stocked a hundred questions in my sleep. Starting with the objects in my sight, I might have begun with "What is this?" and "What is that?" but I knew better than to pester him like a prattling child. I determined to use my time more wisely, to obtain his answer on more important things.

"John?" I asked timidly as we sat quietly by candlelight, I sewing and he mixing some elements in jars and bowls, which I dared not examine too closely for fear he would stop and I'd see nothing more at all.

"Yes?" he replied without pause in his task.

"Are you Christian?"

"Ask nothing of me and we shall both be safer," he replied smoothly.

Heartened by his lack of displeasure and, truly, by the distraction of his task, I pressed on. "When you told me in the Spring that I were not fit—not suitable for the nunnery, referred you to...yesterday? For also you had said that such things are actually common there..."

"Nay, what occurred yesterday is merely the brook that would lead you to the ocean lying within, would you but follow it."

I pondered this, for to me it had a grim sound. "A sea of sin?"

"Aye, such you would name it, no doubt," he said with a sigh.

"And you?" I asked, still more timidly.

He paused then, and looked at me as if only now aware we had been speaking. A look of unmistakable tenderness crossed his face. "Why does a proper Christian child ask such a thing of an evil sinner such as myself, Wicked John Blue? Eh? Do you not fear falling in line with me behind old Beelzebub?"

"I ask only, I'll decide on the morrow what to believe."

He laughed then, to my pleasure, and to my further surprise at my pleasure. "Fair enough, withal," he said, and lapsed into quiet for a moment, his fingers now moving drowsily as they continued their task. "I speak of the other desires and strange qualities within your heart and your days, of which you daren't even whisper into your own ear in the dead of night, so outlandish and so matching in quality are they to all that which is outlined as sin by your learned teachers. Admit these to me, or all further speech is fruitless."

I frowned at the needle in my hand. "All mortals are filled with secret sins..."

"I speak of ones that set you apart, that you know to be different from what your cousins and companions feel. Speak with candor or speak not at all."

I sat awhile quietly now, watching my needle move. "Could you mean such as that I seem to find it harder to obey...?"

"'Tis a start. Why is that, do you think?"

I shrugged then, "A stubborn pride..."

"Whence arises that?"

"'Tis simply my evil nature to turn my ear from God, and I must struggle always to turn it back, whereas others seemingly question not, regardless of their actions."

"What question you?"

"Oh, many things," I said, sighing in grave discomfort. "Why things must be so, why the good suffer as much as the cruel, why God created such evil children, and yet He is perfect. It seems when I am told a thing a demon stands always at my side and whispers questions in my ear, and thrusts forward words to me which seem the truth...but cannot be."

"And this demon who speaks to you—how sounds his voice?"

I snorted then. "I do not hear his voice as I hear yours, if that is what you mean."

"Does he speak with one voice or many?" he asked of me as if I'd said naught.

I was tempted to claim ignorance of the drift of his questions, yet I did not, for such I knew would be the end of our specch altogether. "One, I suppose—'tis more like a feeling that comes with his words..."

"What feeling is that?"

Now I shifted with still greater unease. "'Tis indeed a demon, for although the feelings may be sweet or funny, they are always wrong and full of sin..." I paused, and looked with care at him for sign of shock or ridicule or any such expression. Seeing none, I saw I must continue. "When I was a girl, sometimes he would whisper of events I could not know, and they later happened or proved true. Now...now when I pray, my thoughts sometimes wander...and I might think my heart is full of love for God and for the saints and the sweet Virgin, and yet my thoughts clothe that love in profane images and dreams. I return again to myself and find that much time has passed, of which I was not aware. This is the Devil's work, is it not?" I found myself whispering, so overcome with dread was I.

He sat still for a moment, then I saw suddenly that he was much moved. "Heed you his words?" he asked at last.

I shrugged again, wishing much to minimize this subject, for word after word, sentence after sentence of my speech was purest blasphemy, sufficient each in themselves to bring me sternest censure and possibly grievous harm and punishment. Yet, I thought, feeling very shrewd, I could not fashion in my mind's eye John Blue running to Father Patrus with a list of my sins. That thought made me giggle, but with a look from John I smothered my foolishness and hastened to reply. "Most times I strive to ignore him, but there are times when...I am so lonely and hurting, or cannot see rightly the answer to a question, and then his speech is so kindly, and clever, and I must laugh or be comforted; or I so *know* him to be right in his reply, that I do heed him, and act accordingly."

"With what result?"

I listed for him two or three such instances, as when I applied heat and ginger root to my mother's cough and aches when the midwife said otherwise, and she recovered. Then did John ask of this devil's visage, and name, and other questions, so that I was forced into thinking on the matter, not with loathing and morbid melancholy as before, half fearing to peer beyond the next thought and yet drawn strongly onward against my will, but with a calm and relief most pleasant. Slowly I became aware of the presence of this voice, this other self of mine, and yet felt no panic or angry reprobation, but a deepening of the calm which seemed to fill our little space. I found myself answering John Blue's queries without full understanding of question or reply, and yet most naturally. Simple words we spoke, of the simple events of my life before that time, but somehow, through the light that John shone upon them with his inquiries, did these events seem changed to me. Strangely, my own knowing of their true meaning became more apparent, although it had been far from so at the time of their occurence. Once again, for some hours, time was lost into the evening's passage.

When I fully came to myself again, it was quite late. There we sat as before, he with his foot resting up, and holding my hand most warmly. It seemed to me that we had been so for some time. The voice which rose in my mind like bubbles to the top of a dark lake was gone, along with the sleepy, happy, dreamy feeling. Remnants of words and phrases exchanged with John of Blue hovered behind my mind but seemed to say we shall wait, float awhile longer, do not trouble yourself with us.

I was innocent at that time of my life, and not one to seek out flirtation. And yet the sea within me lapped in a newly risen tide about the shores of my mortal being. It whispered to my hesitant and yearning ears that the man I saw before me did love me somehow—but with such a love! As I looked at him, the face of the Virgin floated again betwixt us. In a sudden, unaccountable conviction, I felt I had just then been speaking with Her again...or was this only dream stuff from the morning?

"I cannot bring to mind, John Blue," I said with difficulty, "if I related to you what came to pass in the Moire?" When he did not reply, but only gazed steadfastly, I plunged into my account, holding back no particulars. As I spoke, in another strange, sudden flash came the knowledge that I was indeed changed. I now viewed that vast inner ocean within my soul—comprised of my feelings and my visions and all my other peculiar secret things—as somewhat in need of protection rather than expungement. Protection from the scrutiny of outsiders, of course—not that of John Blue. I idly wondered if I dwelt now under a demon's sway, yet was I strangely resigned and indifferent to this possibility.

I concluded, speaking finally of the words of the Virgin about a mortal in need of my return, and I looked at him then sharply. With the third of those quick flashes of knowing, I felt this mortal to be none other than John Blue himself. I knew not what to think or say, and looks full of wondrous meaning beyond the reach of any words passed between us. I found myself pressing his hand with both of mine, and then I bowed my head and pressed it to my lips, and saw my tears fall and splash upon it. A great heart-grief then burst upon me and within me, and I knew not its source. John raised my face and stroked my hair, and kissed my forehead with sweet solemnity, and murmured words of blessing and comfort. I clung about his neck and he tenderly nursed me as if I were a weak babe, and spoke words to provide for my safety, and told me I must sleep, and I did.

Early next morn I arose quietly and moved about like a mouse as he slept. Oft I paused to gaze with wonder at his face and form, yet I did not dawdle to pick up each tiny curious object round me, but otherwise set the grate and emptied the night jar and set about to put the place aright before he woke, as would befit a dutiful woman.

He was cold and quiet when he rose, and yet as we went about our tasks, he conveyed by look and touch that his displeasure was not with me, but rather with his weary hurting bones, with the cold, oddly smelling breeze flowing in through the open window and door. The heavy, warm and quiet air, soft, fragrant and pregnant with dreams, of the night and day before was vanished, and its taste was bittersweet in our mouths.

Then came the moment when, in my mix of woman and child, I timidly but helplessly held to him and asked to remain with him and not return. Indeed, I offered myself as his servant, handmaid or woman. He held me then at some distance, with a firm hand I did not venture to undermine, and said with a strange and tender amusement, "Ere we may lie thigh to thigh, my child, must pass a certain time and manifold events the shape of which is known by none, including me. Return to your place, and bide your time and peace, and strengthen your heart-sight by the means I have laid down for you, for it will light your way. Say naught to anyone. Do this, and you shall be safe until my return."

And, although strong was my sadness and my love for him, I made no try to win him with guile or threat, but acquiesced with trembling heart and full trust that he was right.

As I stepped over my own threshold once again, darker than ever before, it seemed, my mind was in constant rehearsal preparing for inquiry into my absence. I stopped short, however, for there sat my mother in uncharacteristic repose before the gutted hearth, and her eyes brushed me over with no regard in them. Bella then ran to me, her unwashed face a bit too cold and ashen for her health. Then she uttered words which served to justify my mother's despair and change the course of my life at once: "The plague is here," she whispered, and clung to me in fear.

Five

'Twas a natural thing to sweep the land, this black death. 'Tis no more than what will happen to any kind of creature when their numbers are too many or their misery is too great. 'Tis a wonder only that the human creature, one that habitually dams its few means to joy and comfort at their source, is not continually plagued with such curses, but such is the luck of the race.

I knew therefore some causes for any particular person to inhale the Death by the time it began to appear along the looping peddler's route of my travels: despair being foremost, followed by all the tedious but pertinent qualities afflicting more and more folk in all lands: poverty, unjust labor, hunger, cold, and impure water and diet. All these stemmed in their turn from a cause claimed by many as the cure: the utterly unnatural and spirit-destroying dictates of the Christian church.

Perhaps wrongly did I consider knowledge of these truths a shield against them. Perhaps the poisonous bitterness I deemed wrapped and discarded two years prior I instead carried within me along the way, festering and waiting within my soul. Regardless of the reason, regardless of the several precautions I took when I once saw the sweep of this event, I found myself stricken.

I was at that time in the vicinity of the Abbey of St. Mary's, and near the time of the Autumn rites. Perceiving the sudden purple swellings beneath my arms to be the cause or corollary of my recent lethargy, I prepared to remain hidden in my caravan and nurse myself as best I could, or die. I cared not much either way, for the despondency of this disease was a river that sucked into itself all the common darker tributaries of my soul, bitterness, melancholy and weariness withal, until all formed a single torrent.

However, next day I roused myself to prepare a note for my Elizabeth with news of my fate. With great effort I climbed astride my mare for the short way to town, but I turned aside partway there, going instead to the Abbey which was closer, as my strength was short and I did not fancy falling and dying by the road.

I do not recall much after that decision, for I fell at the gate and did not awaken for some time.

I shall never forget, though, the face like the flame of the candle which burned my eyes when I awoke: that of my little St. Catherine. Six months had passed since I had seen her last, and I had almost succeeded in banishing her from my mind, but as I gazed at her busying herself over the succeeding weeks of my convalescence, I permitted the scenes and emotion of our previous discourse to visit me in my delirium. 'Tis rare indeed to recover from the Death, and I attribute much of my survival to the faint hope rekindled by her face as much as to her careful ministrations to me.

Long and hard were those days for her. The place grew quieter and quieter as the sisters and the poor who'd found refuge there fled or died. 'Tis only the stoniest heart that does not relent at the constant sight and touch of such a one as Cathy, who flinched not at the foulest stench, and bathed the filthiest putrescence with the tenderness of a lover.

Knowing that she ministered to me not anonymously but in secret familiarity was the source of even deeper emotion. For, although betimes I believe that I've blustered, drunk and slept with half the folk of the continent and a fair portion of those of other lands to boot, I number those with a knowledge of the full scope of identity on my fingers. Long ago I donned the skin of the chameleon, wearing brown and reflecting only that which need be seen to ensure my survival. This policy left body sated and safe, and yet with freedom of movement to practice the true arts and pleasures demanded by my spirit, albeit in secrecy. Being fond of solitude and delighting in my craft withal, I paid with small grudge the price of loneliness, for always there were those few souls scattered about to whom I could truly turn my full face and voice. However, as all price is prone to be, I found it increased at this time. I had been honored to receive and contain much wisdom over the course of my life; perhaps it was pride in this which had masked the creature-need for common knowing and affection, and so permitted it to fester and flower, finally, with the Black Rose of Death. Delirium and weakness finally brought this stony, pained and starving pride to its knees, as my eyes fastened on Cathy's form as a lone anchor within a stormy world now shrunk to consist solely of my pain, a few bare walls, floor, water cup, and cot.

We did not speak much, because of her work, my illness and the not-lessened need for political care. Of course, few words are needed between those who speak with eyes, mind and heart and not just tongue. The frightened, angry child I'd fished from the Moire had a steadiness within: her eyes opened deeply into her and vouched for her initiation into the world that was her own soul, as per my instruction half a year prior. Some nights I awoke to find her curled sleeping beside my cot, weeping silently but most piteously in her grief, fear, and heavy weariness. With heart in throat at these times I gave her comfort by touching and stroking her hair, which above all things within my power did ease her.

The time came when I pulled my feet fully from the next

world and back into this one, and knew that I should live. Coming from an easeful sleep of some two days, I was surprised at the quiet in the air, the absence of reverberation through the wall or floor. Feeling a small but sure surge of strength in my bones, I rose and weakly crossed the room.

I knew the day was bright, but indeed I was blinded stepping from my sickroom to the hall, where the sun shone at his height and without obstruction. I leaned unsteadily against the wall and covered my eyes momentarily, and when they cleared I opened them to a lovely sight indeed.

There sat Catherine in a courtyard astream with the sun's light, leaning with eyes closed and neck and arms bared to his rays, for there was no wind. Her eyes opened and fell upon me, and a slow smile found her lips and eyes, and jumped across the way to my mouth, which seemed to creak as it performed the unaccustomed exercise.

Soon she was at my side, her strong little arms and shoulders propping me as I moved to the sun like a bee to pollen.

" 'Tis very quiet," I said.

"We are alone here, the others have gone," she replied.

"What, all dead?"

"Nay, though mostly so. Yestereve a rider summoned the last of the sisters to aid a noble family some miles from here."

I moved into the sun's benign gaze, and 'twas indeed a rebirth of sorts. I clawed at my collar as I sank down to a spot across from where she'd sat, and as I leaned back I could fain hear my skin cry out in ecstasy in a thousand tiny voices. I sat quietly for a while, opening myself to the sun's Divinity, feeling him enter me, feeling Strength, his companion, enter alongside, coupling potently with my own vital force. Lovers they were within me, their seed to become my new life. Cathy resumed her place, and we sat in silence.

"Theresa?" I asked then.

"She has gone with the others," she replied.

"I am glad she was not stricken," I said, parting my lids just so as to see her visage.

"Yes, she is dear to me."

I smiled again. "So, you are not lovers."

She touched my foot with one of hers, smiling too. " 'Tis lucky for me I do not relish secrecy. I could say the day is bright and you would thence recite my breakfast meal."

We sat in silent enjoyment. A shutter banged and she started, and a faint veil of old fear passed over her face, one which only now did I realize had been there from before.

"What do you fear?" I asked, covering her toes with a nudge in my turn, to prevent her dissembling on my account.

"There is a band hereabouts..." she admitted, "one of great desperation..."

Now I understood much more. "This hastened the departure of your companions."

She was silent in acquiescence.

"I am surprised," I said, "that you were left here thus alone."

"They wished me to come with them, for you could have been left with water and food beside you by that time..."

The dark, dark brown of her eyes was a pool far within forest's shade as she held me in them, floating, floating on her deepened love for me. The strength of the peasant twined with some bloodline spark from long ago, and I saw then almost palpably the exquisite creature she would become shortly, very soon indeed.

"We shall leave shortly, by nightfall, my love," I said.

"They left no mule," she said tensely.

"We shall manage. Think no more on it. Open yourself again. More. Exhale your fear—so. We gain more by one hour in the arms of the Sun than in three rushing and straining in fear. I promise we shall be safe." I had indeed hastily devised a plan in event of need.

Her face relaxed to my satisfaction, I followed suit, and for a quiet time we sat and basked.

Next forenoon we were sitting comforted and quiet in my conveyance, supping hungrily. The night's sojourn was tedious but uneventful, we had slept late, and now I could sense almost full recovery for us both.

"Will you take yourself home until the sisters' return, then?" I asked of her, seeing it was time for this issue.

She paused for a mere instant, but I saw her gather herself tensely. "They are dead," she said, not meeting my eyes. Yet, this was not grief felt nor deferred, but something else.

"What do you plan then?"

Another pause, full, pregnant. No eyes. "I know not." Eating still, but slowing.

"What do you desire?" I asked with all patience.

At that, she rose and busied herself somewhat brusquely.

"I might stay with 'Becca for a time...or venture to join the others." This followed by silence, save the clattering.

"Is that answer to my query?" I asked, my heart grown soft and warm at her effort.

She finished her work and paused to regard a fingernail in sudden fascination. "I am due to take my vows on Michael-mas. Should the world still run by then," she added darkly.

"Methinks you belong rather on a tight-rope in the circus, so skillfully do you balance 'twixt worlds."

She shrugged, switching hands to inspect the other. "It has been easy. I love their God no less for knowing more of His true nature and my own."

"History would be different indeed could more folk ac-complish that feat." With pleasure I watched a flush caress her neck.

"I keep my own counsel," she added after the silence pushed her.

"I am pleased," I said with some craft.

"'Twas not done to please you, but only to survive with some meaning to my life. You were not there, if you may recall," only daring to sharpen her words, not her voice.

"Do you see no merit in this time spent growing in the truth, independent of my sway?"

Then she lowered her hands, still remaining, though, with her back to me. "Aye," she said with quiet emotion.

I waited a moment, in truth to steady my voice as well as any other reason. "And what do you desire now?" I asked again.

"What does it matter if my desire remain constant upon you?" she replied quickly. "So that I might say so, and you may say nay yet again, and still know yourself my master?"

A keen shaft was this she'd shot, and it found my heart all too readily. I rose then and, stepping behind her, placed my hands on her shoulders, and my mouth to touch her hair. "I must hear the words, Cathy, to prevent just such abuse," I said with a sweet restraint.

She steadied herself with care. "Aye, I would come with you, John Blue, though it were to the rack and Hell beyond, and thus would my answer be after ten years, and not merely six months."

Then I turned her to me, and with all slowness and care I touched her face and held her chin, and kissed her fully on her mouth at some length. We almost fell, as a result of my weakness and her womanly swooning response. This caused a giddy mirth to rise in us both. How her eyes did shine, and how quickly did her lips learn and seek mine again, and for a time we stood leaning against the wall in great tenderness, kissing and touching each other.

"I would take you with me this time," I said. Then did she cling about my neck. I was glad for my weakness, for I was strongly tempted to discard the plan I had been forming and carry her to bed. Instead I murmured most gently to her ear that our love must not be consummated for some little time yet. I saw on her face some slight disappointment mingled with a greater relief: girls of her station must, by the rule, see their dreams abandoned or crushed far before their blooming, and 'twas a recognized privilege for one such as Cathy to be permitted to fondle and court for a time. Then we resumed our places, though she maneuvered always to lay a hand or knee on me, for she was a most warm and affectionate creature withal.

We ventured next day into a world much changed. I had known from before how this plague did oft infest a place and well nigh destroy it while leaving another place a day's ride thence virtually untouched. The former had occurred herewith. Ghostly silent were the roads, farms and dwellings standing in the morning's mist. By mid-afternoon's slanting rays we had in hand two sturdy head of horses, which seemed relieved to be taken in hand once again, and various and sundry supplies and foodstuffs for our journey, all free and ours for the taking. Determining on a morning departure, we dined in a field at the furthest of our ranging, drank heavily of a bottle of fine, potent ale, and our spirits became quite elevated. This was necessary, as the horrors confronting our noses and eyes as we stumbled upon corpses through the day's pilferings had succeeded in quite unnerving us. Seeing folk lying scattered about unburied like animals, mouths and eyes open as oft as not, with expressions of agony and terror yet grimacing their features, produced an effect on the senses somehow more sinister than when the dead are confined to the battlefield or sickroom. Making our way to the caravan that dusk we were quite oblivious though, singing and jesting over the incongruous and macabre sights we had stumbled across. Much did I taunt her for this conduct, so unbecoming to a novitiate. Most beautiful she was, this jewel of my age.

Some two weeks later we reached the house of my dear Elizabeth. Full with feeling was our reunion, for in truth I had avoided her for two years, since our son was lost to us. I saw by her face that she immediately comprehended my purpose and feeling for Cathy, and she warmly embraced the girl. The resemblance between the two was uncanny, regardless of the difference between them of more than two-score years.

I had kept silent to Cathy regarding our destination, and regarding the paths of thinking slowly being cleared in my mind. Truly, she was so distracted by all the strange new sights and sounds of our travels, and by the learning of various other elements of my trade, as well as more general, if secret, lore and advice I was gradually disclosing, that she cared little. Her hard-won trust and constancy, her effort, most plain to Elizabeth and myself, to curb her natural childish exuberance and curiosity and behave soberly, in the face of her recent losses and harsh and fearsome trials, finally won us entirely. A fortnight after our arrival we sat down to answer the questions in her eyes.

Slowly and carefully did Lizzie and I reveal more to her of what I had begun disclosing the previous spring. I related how I had in truth known and dreamed of her in my nightly travels since before her birth, and thence knew to watch for and mark her presence when I began catching glimpses of her at her mother's side some ten years before this. I had not known what role she would play in my life's events, particularly as a nun! This latter development had seeded my speculations with no end of bafflement and frustration. Yet I had known her to be "one of us" in all potentiality, with talents and qualities most unique and endearing. We spoke of the tiny, tiny numbers of those mortal souls now living and forming a family, a word with meaning independent of the usual confining definition of that word: This family is one of the soul. Our family is given to envisioning and to cultivating the inner and outer powers of the mind, often to the sacred and profane arts, to medicine, and to the disclosure of truth to the degree and of a nature appropriate to the grasp of the particular listener. We are high in integrity, and not given to slavish greed or dull petty spite, and yet under the tedious weight of unfruitful and meaningless labor, when there falls no sunlight on the blossoms of spirit and mind, we often wither and perish long before others. Our kind are more tempted by gluttony and lechery and any indulgence of the senses, and the more unhappy and frustrated of our kind can travel great distances along these paths. Some of our number naturally find their way into churchly service and devotion, but we can engender much friction against the sterner dictates and restrictions of same, until and unless the inner wisdom is heard and followed primarily.

We spoke of the true work of this family: that of reminding others of the knowledge already coiled and latent within each heart, this knowledge being that we seek ourselves through time and circumstance like the hunter his prey, whether backward or forward it matters not, passing some places or years in the flicker of a dream, and lingering in others. All of Life, in all her many shades and forms, material and seemingly less so, consisting of this Hunt, with a glowing vision of the Future brushing shoulders with a searing event long past, and with these two joined closer together than either yesterday or tomorrow by the comprehensions and yearnings of the Human soul. "And who is this self we seek, and what is the meaning of this Hunt?" enquired Cathy, her eyes bright and avid upon us. And we laughed then, and said that this was the greatest mystery of all, and that its proof must lie in its discovery.

We are not to be confused with the followers of Satan or even of the old pagan gods, each group of which holds many more in number than we do. Nor are we primarily among the learned secular, for we grow impatient with dry and dusty tomes. We tend to stay among the middling folk in all obscurity, and listen to the trees' whisper and to our hearts' love for each other, in contented secrecy. Thus we can often accomplish much with simple advice and remedies, with a heightened quality in our work, in the hand we extend in friendship, in the beauty we may cultivate, though it might be merely in a single square yard of garden. Thus do we also avoid persecution, for carelessly do we avow Christ, and why not? There is nothing quoted as proceeding directly from his lips which contravenes our beliefs; such occurs only among his priests and followers.

Cathy was much moved to hear these things—as were we in their relating. With the subject of persecution, Lizzie and I paused and grew somber and sad, however, and we each took the other's hand. With a sigh and a tear, we related our son's birth some twenty years prior, and of his growth into a man of piercing ken and passionate spirit. He had a thirst for the world in all its known glory, and spent years in the east and in other lands distant and unknown even to his old father. Upon his return, he was grown too large in spirit for the narrow society comprising his birth land, and would not heed admonishment to secrecy and discretion. He came into conflict with a certain merchant of some standing, a man in alliance with the local papal authority. The conflict became personal, and Paul's pride became hopelessly entangled: he was finally taken, grievously tortured, and killed, for he would not repent.

Much time did we take then, speaking with laughter and tears comingled, at Cathy's tender coaxing, of his qualities and sundry details of his life. This eased my heart, for I had been overcome with bitterness upon his death and for these two years, to the extent of estranging myself from my beloved Liz.

Finally I confessed, with much pain and halting tongue, my long-harbored fear that there were some action or advice to prevent this calamity, which I, in negligence, had omitted. I received much comfort from both my loving friends on this matter, and my heart was much eased.

Now we came to the centerpiece of our meeting, and Lizzie kissed us both and parted from us into the other room. I took Cathy's hand in mine, in our accustomed way, and told her my thoughts.

Lizzie kept herself primarily by spinning and weaving I said, and also by selling eggs and cheese, and by other sundry crafts and means. Also, she ministered as local midwife. Those who could be trusted also were recommended into her hands for healing of a more secret and esoteric variety, as well as for maladies and wounds of the heart and fortunes. She it was who had taught me discretion when, as a raw youth, I first attended and then succeeded my father on his rounds, and began scraping into frequent trouble through the untamed and misunderstood nature of my own power.

I proposed that, for one year after Spring, Cathy might dwell with Lizzie and reap of this living harvest of human lore and wisdom. Lizzie would keep and hold her as a daughter, and such a daughter as Cathy would we have welcomed. She would be free to depart before that date, of course, or to remain past, but the choice she might also have then would be to take stock of what feeling might remain in her for me. Should it be modulated into an affection as toward a father or uncle with the blooming of her womanhood and the means of making a place for herself through what she had learned, then so should the love between us remain sacrosanct unto the heart and not the flesh, so as it now was.

If, however, her present sensual ardor and full passion for me should remain and heighten with her age, we would consummate it then and thereafter, and I would hold both her and Lizzie thenceforth equally in my hand and heart as beloved mates.

With nature's blessing and consent we would be fortunate to usher one or more souls through her body into this world. I was almost overcome in speaking on this thing, for most strange and gifted would those children be, yet strong and dexterous upon the earth withal.

I was pleased to see Cathy so full with excitement and happiness that she seemed well nigh to bursting. Then she grew quiet, drew her face moistly close to mine, and inquired as to whether it would be wiser to cleave unto me now, for in my absence she would fear the loss of me before the year was past, and hence the loss of all our unborn young. Who can exceed the sweetly devious and compelling charms of a virgin, fully roused in heart and flesh, hellbent with determination purely innocent, yet lit all round with flame?

But I was prepared and determined, and I triumphed over sore temptation, and satisfied her somewhat with kisses and caresses rough and smooth, and words of explanation.

How has it come to be, I reflected, my passion shot with anger as I stood with them upon my departure, that humankind has become so twisted as to assign the lowest motive and sensibility to womankind? As we three stood clasping in a ring, their waists so warm and breathing in my arms, and their sweet sublime smells arising to my nostrils; as my heart did swell to accommodate their blessings and love for the coming several months; and as images of all my greatest fears about their fates in this cruel and low society gained sway in my momentary weakness, I felt, finally, simple weariness with the seemingly impossible burden of explanation. I slowed my mind and found that center point from which all life springs, and simply felt my blessing and my fortune, to so rise beyond the misery of my time.

Six

Spark of darkness, midnight's glow
One above sees one below
Always love redeems the loss
Lower eyes and reach across

Rose of death joins dark and light
One with eyes sees one with sight
Always love redeems the loss
Lower masks and reach across

Hope sustains while patience burns
One who needs sees one who yearns
Always love redeems the loss
Lower walls and reach across

Thus went the words chanted over my head on the night fantastic and ecstatic, on which I joined with John of Blue at last.

I was then full in my womanhood, some fifteen years of age. In truth, I looked back upon the child I had been but two years prior with kindness and forbearance: for such blossoms are cultivated by the learning and wisdom that I had shared with Lizzie.

Unclothed and supine, I lay upon the magic stone, limbs spread in the magic star. Above me, heaven's stars were timid in night's canopy, for torchlight challenged them all round about me. At my head stood Lizzie, lover, mother, sister and friend, with her hands gently among my hairs twining and stroking in affection and reassurance, for despite all preparation, the excitement, fear and desire were coursing so strong in my blood that she sensed I wondered at my containment of them.

A dozen faces, some strange, some dear, circled us in movement to the chant. With each concluding phrase, they reached across my body to touch fingers together. Four gently held me by wrist and ankle, but in caress and not in bond. Over me lay the virgin's white, in the sweetest gauze that had ever graced my skin. I saw my desire reflected fire-like in all faces and eyes, and I knew myself to be blessed indeed with beauty fine.

The months gone by since John had taken me in his arms and kissed me, had been like as to a dream. All ways of plant and rock, of liquid, fire and air, and also the ways of shrewder thought and speech and ways of discourse had Lizzie taught me. And in our bed at night, 'twas not long in our acquaintance before my thirsty hands and lips, my heart spilling its hunger through my eyes to hers as we lay nose to nose, had found her river leading in, and had flowed thereon with her blessing and her need. My fires she had stoked as well, and all to my delight had I found that assuagement strangely only built them higher yet, with passage of the months sweet yet torturous indeed. I was hurting for John by now, with his face mingled more and more within all of my imaginings, and with his name whispered 'twixt Lizzie and myself in our times of passion as often as not. Yet I had resisted quenching my flames in dull carnality with the local lads, well-meaning though they seemed, and my virgin force was yet intact and ripe to offer John, and, by his taking of it, to those we loved.

The soul stands apart from earth, and words forget their sense, when the ring is formed. Soon I found my mind loosen from its holdings, and I fancied each touch from loving hand to send a spirit all its own into my blood to join the others' coursing. Likewise did our friends gasp and start upon their touching me to feel the force of all my love move into them. Strange vivid waking dreams passed before my eyes, as like to my private imaginings, potent enough though they were, as the open sea to tiny brook. Other faces I saw float above the visages of those I thought I knew, and I would have been hard pressed to say which one was real in that moment's heat.

Then full soft and sudden the voices and movement were stilled and all stood around me in a tense anticipation. Lizzie was gone. I raised my head to look down between my breasts, for there I knew John would appear. The sight I saw caused me, without volition, to struggle to reclaim my limbs, pulling against the hands which now clasped me firm. Dizzy and uncertain as I was, thus was the sight I saw rendered the more horrible. A figure towered silently, without motion, at my feet. Smeared with midnight blue, it had a wolf's face and arms, and I could clearly see the silver of its fur and the white of its fangs. Hard and huge was its phallus in readiness for me, and as my eyes beheld this sight, and my struggling was to no avail, I released a moan of purest terror, which was echoed in moans of a different nature around me, and whispers and sighs.

With craft such as any fanged creature uses when it stalks its prey, this being slowly raised one knee, and then its mate, to kneel between my feet upon my stone, all the while with eyes pinning mine as predators will do. I shut my eyes in some hope that this dream would dissipate. I was chilled anew, flooded with panic to feel the creature's paw affix itself to my fragile covering, and slowly draw it down and off my body, leaving four close trails of sensation, where its claws had gently scraped across my belly.

Was this truly my John? The eyes were black and shaded beneath the jutting mask. Moreover, looking into them, I felt no familiarity, only an endless chasm of dreams dark and vivid at once. In addition, my wandering mind seemed to lose what daylit sense it possessed at this time, and I truly wondered where I was and what transpired. All that I had heard of demons and black magic, the thousand tales and warnings I'd been told as a girl, seemed enfleshed about me. Would I be betrayed after all?

Wild and rank odors assailed me as this creature peered at me, bending closer. Now I could perceive John's beard below the fur; how eagerly did my eyes seek his familiar mouth, and with what renewed terror did they see it curled in the smile of a stranger. Then truly did something in my spirit snap, and I possessed no further control over my wild-running thoughts. "Betrayal..." I heard whispered, once and then many times. The creature raised its paw to me again, and I saw the glint of a dagger; I shut my eyes fast and screamed and struggled with utter abandon, sure that my soul and body were forfeit to the Dark One himself. I felt then the fine, cool trace of knife on flesh, a deliberate draw down center from breast to groin, agony hard on its heels. I opened my streaming eyes to see this dark creature scoop its paws into my gut, ladle out my still living entrails, and offer them to the Moon brightly beaming above us, and howl, and howl, as my blood dripped down and streamed across my sides...

I heard my name as if from far off...and again, and again. I returned, whence I knew not, to the present time and place. Still I lay flat on my back, still I felt the hands on me, still I heard the fire-snaps of torches and saw their dancing light behind my lids. My belly seemed filled with bees a-buzz, my skin's hairs were raised all round about my flesh. I was frightened to breathe for fear the pain from my ravaged gut would return.

But I heard my name again, in a modulation sweetly familiar and harkening back to an unremembered time of light. Slowly I opened my eyes, and saw quite close the face of John of Blue. He wore no mask, and at the tender concern

I saw splayed across his features, I felt a small part of my pressing panic drain away. Yet I could still hear and see the things of that other time and place, most especially the blue-cloaked and hooded figure, which I felt to somehow actually be my John of Blue.

I opened mouth to speak; he touched my lips with his fingertips.

"Release them," he said. "Let them follow or remain, as they wish."

Once again, and for the last time, I stood at a crossroads. Believe him and obey? or beg to be released? I did not understand his words and yet as I searched his eyes so close to mine I found further calm. Closing my eyes, I spoke to the shadow-forms I still felt pressing in all round the table. "You are free," I said, "Follow or remain, as you wish."

I heard murmurs and rustlings, as eerie as the fields of corn at night, from those forms, and from the living ones present with me. Slowly the air thinned and cleared, and when some minutes later I opened my eyes again, I beheld merely John's face framed by the fresh midsummer night, and only those living stood once more clear and familiar about me.

Slowly, slowly came a dawning remembrance of this night as it truly was, my wedding night. Slowly did my captor and myself share a smile between us, sipping from it as from the Cup itself. I perceived then that 'twas his hand resting upon my belly causing such sensation, and suddenly I was visited by strong desire, of a kind that came like a hammered knife between my legs, inflaming my womb and all my womanly parts with a vehemence that made me gasp in astonishment, lit with delight. Naturally John perceived and understood what passed, and I saw the familiar lechery that I knew from so long ago spread about his features; however, it was transfigured this night by finer emotion, his love for me.

At once the air dancing live around us raised its pitch still higher, and I heard chatter and giggles and sighs and breathing from the friends and witnesses gathered there. And then began the mating, starting with a kiss most tender, then passionate, as his palm massaged my womb with peculiar effectiveness straight through the skin of my belly. Now I struggled again, but playfully and without volition; and as his mouth and hands moved about my body soft and roughly, quick and slow, but always with a knowing of it, always with his eyes for me to fasten on, sometimes with burning unsustainable in truth, and my womanforce mounted and reached and climbed to heights unendurable. At last and at last he took my thighs in hand and opened them further, and bent and drank of the cup nestled between them; and yet still did he, through movement asserted and withdrawn, teasing and loving, prevent my release! Now I groaned and writhed most whorishly, and begged and pleaded, and the others laughed and stroked me more boldly, and spoke profanities which I lambishly repeated, and I kissed and grasped whatever was offered me, and finally began to weep somewhat.

Then he raised himself to fullest height, and grand indeed he looked, and full was I with pride. "Shall it be done?" he roared in great good humor.

"Aye!" they answered in full voice equally, and silence fell again.

"Do you, Catherine of Middlelea, offer this your maidenhood, not solely to myself and to the Spirit, but to all gathered here, and through the Spirit to all whom we know and love, and this all willingly?"

"Oh, aye," I sighed, and the others laughed softly at the need in my voice, but I did not mind. Then silence fell yet again, and his eyes locked with mine at last, and he took himself in hand and mounted me, and tenderly and firmly penetrated, and after one small cramp like as to the bite of flea, I was lost in pleasure. This time silence stayed in the air all full with solemnity, except for our tiny creature-sounds of love. Still he played out the time, and eternity passed before us, nose to nose, seeing visions in our eyes; he pressed and held and pulled from me the cry of death. All hands were on us at that time, and I felt our spirits racing back and forth between us all, and my force was pulled out from me and drunk by them.

Then, with my cry, a great shout arose from them, and merrymaking broke loose, though all quiet were my John and I, still gazing into each other's eyes. Then my hands and feet were released, and I wrapped about him; it seemed to me that no one nor nothing else existed nor ever had nor would, save the love we shared.

The Long Reach

The Play

Seven

There is a well-lit room in a high place, overlooking a broad valley striped with barley crops and vineyards. Sunset is splashed across half the sky for these few minutes. The darkening blue of the other half blanches the brown of the outside wall into bluish chalk.

Inside the room the lamplight is yellow. There is order here, all in its place. The room smells old, the things in it have the tattered, precious look of antiquity, and this is reflected in the white hair of the figure sitting motionless on the porch, watching the sun descend.

It is very, very still. One looks for the pulse in the throat of the old man, for the light rise and fall of his chest, so quietly does he sit. The bird in its cage in the corner sits puffed on one foot, beak tucked under its wing, its visible eye trembling with dreams, but shut.

Softly the door-covering is moved aside and a woman steps in. She carries a tray with food, and its aroma stirs the air. This woman is dark, about 40, and she has a pleasant body. Firm and smooth, strong and graceful. Her face is pleasant too, although it is a closed kind of face. One wouldn't know if this woman were kind or stern, or what mood she might be in, just by looking at her face. She moves quietly and treats the objects she touches with respect, but this could be merely out of duty, since she is a slave. The bird awakens from its dream and watches her, its feathers still ruffled, one leg still hidden.

The woman turns up the lamp, moves some things around. Then she goes to the old man. As soon as she kneels before him, placing one hand over his, and looks up into his face, we know it is not mere duty that makes her movements so full of care and gentleness.

The old man has not reacted to her presence. He still gazes out over the field. His eyes are black, and although they are not rheumy, they are quite absorbed.

Another degree of darkness falls as she waits, gently stroking his hand with a very tiny motion.

Finally his eyes lower to hers. Animation slowly seeps into his face, although this is a subtle process, steam rising on a winter's morn. A softening, a coloring, and he is all there, looking at her.

They share the same moist, inward-turning smile. Slowly he places his hand over hers and squeezes. She leans to him and places her lips on his fingers, kisses them softly, slowly. He raises her hand to his mouth and presses it there. Suddenly there is some inner tremor, he capsizes beneath some emotional wave, and shuts his eyes. Quickly she raises herself closer to him, places her face very near his. He almost turns away, but she makes him look into her eyes again.

Many emotions swim and flash in his eyes now, and she reads them all, one by one. She strokes the lines of his face, touches her lips to his. At last he subsides, and releases her hand to slowly stroke her hair, her face. His brow clears as she draws near for a longer kiss.

After a while they are draped in a blanket of darkness, and the newborn stars are blinking sleepily up in the night. She helps him get to his feet. He holds his clawed right hand close to his chest. His right leg is fairly useless too, and it gets dragged a little as they make their way in. He was once a big, strong extravagant man, but now he is contained and a little stooped. With her in her prime, exuding health, they balance out now to be nearly equal in strength.

"Do you know what happened today?" she asks him. "Philip has declared that anyone not in favor of his proposal is to be considered in Alex's camp, that there can be no middle ground, 'no time to spare' is how he put it." The old man grunts and motions with his claw. They settle him into his chair, she draws his table near, and he scribbles something on his slate. She glances at it between her other motions.

"Yes, he's an idiot, but the others are afraid. There was another robbery in that district, and the holidays may be very quiet this year."

The old man scribbles again. There is a shock of white as she tosses aside his robe to expose his bad leg, and begins rubbing a salve into it. She lifts her head to glance at his slate when he's finished. "Well, that's what Paul is suggesting and I guess most of the others would rather go with him, but they're just not sure it's going to be worthwhile. Bend."

The old man scribbles for some minutes now, while the woman rubs and works some flexibility into the leg. Then he stops writing and for some minutes more they concentrate solely on their physical task.

Finished, she gets up and begins moving away. He catches her wrist lightly and then points to his slate. She remembers and stops to read it. "No, I don't remember..." and keeps reading. She becomes absorbed. "This is really true?" she looks at him, and there is a shrewd certainty in his face. "Hm," she says, and her smile holds a pleased respect. "I'll tell Benjamin tonight. If it works out, we'll hold another feast in your honor." He nods once and looks away, satisfied.

She turns away and busies herself with his food tray. He

115

looks back at her, at her thigh and buttocks sheathed in modest blue cotton but very round and near his hand. He caresses her, slowly and sensuously, as if the cotton is fine gold silk. His black eyes flash up to what he can see of her face, but her eyes are closed, her hands still. He looks down again, and some of the muscles in his face relax just a little, his passion contained and speaking through the motion of one strong hand, stroking and kneading her the way he knows she likes it. Their breathing deepens, synchronizes. Just as he slips his hand beneath the cloth, there is a sudden deafening squawk from the parrot, and both of them jump, then laugh.

"Your supper will get cold," she says, pulling away from his hand, but as they part their eyes meet again, so she can show him her desire.

She lowers the blind against the night, and unlatches the parrot's door. It flies and lands on the high back of the old man's chair, eyes the food, and begins chattering and stepping quickly from side to side. The old man immediately hands it a bit, which the woman notices. "Leo!" she complains, and he is pleased with this reaction.

They eat from the same bowls.

They are having a good time tonight, drinking a good bit of wine, laughing, playing around. She talks to him, he writes things back. She tells him he hasn't eaten anything green in a week, pops a seaweed ball into his mouth, saying he cannot stop her, pinning his right arm. He wrenches it free, panting with the struggle. He holds another ball up, motioning to her, and she leans over and sucks it from his fingers. Her mouth is smeared, and he pulls her chin over to him, and licks the food from her face. It tickles and she shrieks with laughter.

A bit falls on his chest, and she parts his collar and buries her face there, licking him clean. As she pulls away, he slides her loose dress down over her shoulders, revealing her beautiful breasts. He dips his fingers in the dessert bowl and smears some on her nipples. More serious now, she moves his tray, shoos away the parrot, and climbs closer to him.

They lie sleeping back to back, joined at the spine. It is a lovely cool midsummer early morning, and the air is gray and moist, the sun already on his way.

Suddenly, Leo is having a nightmare. He moans and twitches, then subsides and is still again, but his eyes move behind their lids.

He opens his eyes. Slowly, with a little effort, he sits up, rubbing them. He sighs and droops a little. She stirs and puts a hand on his knee. "Are you all right?" sleepily.

He doesn't respond, doesn't look at her. She touches him and prompts him a little more, her voice liquid soft and irresistible.

He reaches over and picks up the slate. He places it on his knee and writes for a while as she languidly strokes his back.

He hands it to her. As she reads, he sits motionlessly with his hand over his eyes. A couple of tears slide out from beneath and run down his cheeks.

Her voice is milky with emotion when she finishes reading and gently prompts him to lie back down and against her. He is like her baby now, with his helpless arm as he sighs and relents, allowing her to enfold him. Her voice is a slow river, and he floats slowly downstream as she speaks.

"Why do you let such things prey on you so? Why can you not accept the way things are now? You love me and yet you will not listen to me. The hurt that I felt then is gone, and has been gone for many years. So why then do you act as if it were only yesterday?

"Do you know, I do not think of it when I remember those days? Do you believe me? And this is not because I am afraid to remember, or still hurting. No, it's because the other memories are stronger, the good ones. Do you remember the first time I met you? Do you? I will remind you again. It is one of my best memories.

"My mother and I had just been taken to this house. I was

crying and Neba—remember Neba?—was scolding me. You came into the room, and,..." and here the woman stops a moment, gathering herself silently and motionlessly, before continuing, "and you were so handsome, so big, and your hair was so black and your robe so white, and your voice shook the roof! I was just a little country girl, not even my first menstruation, and I had never seen anyone as big as you, or as fine. How your eyes flashed! When you looked at me, I forgot all my troubles. I still do," and she chokes a little again. He looks up into her face, and they kiss.

"Now let me finish. You asked me something and I didn't answer, just sucked my fingers. Then you and my mother began talking about sweetened bean curd—you wanted her to make you some because Anna had just left, remember? But Neba was arguing with you because it would upset cook. And then—what happened? Oh, yes. Neba doubted whether my mother could even make it well, and I spoke up then and said she certainly could—only one day I had been there and I knew about house politics! Then you said—do you remember?—you said that she must be able to, since she had produced me, and from the look of me my fingers must be sweet indeed. You asked me their flavor, and when I didn't reply, you said you would just have to find out for yourself, and took them in your mouth and sucked them yourself!"

"You don't seem to understand how that helped me."

"I am a slave, Leo. I was your slave. What you did to me happens every day everywhere. And yet, those men think nothing, absolutely nothing, of what they do. Little girl or no, I loved you, I flirted with you and seduced you. I was shocked and hurt by what you did, but the man you sold me to was very, very kind, and I healed very quickly. I have never been beaten, Leo! How many owners would make such careful arrangements as that, and how many slaves instead lie strangled at the bottom of the river?

"I had a good life those 25 years. Sol is a good man and I love him still, but you...I never stopped being yours in my heart. Do you believe me? He knew it. After I came back here and saw you that day, he knew I wanted to be with you again, without my saying a word. It's to his credit that he knew but it speaks to the depth of my feeling for you as well.

"I am remembering a dream I began having just after you sold me. You and I are together in it, but different. We are in a big strange house, and there are many strange things there, and also many big white squares that I have painted strange things on, but they are beautiful and many people are there to see them. I am very anxious and afraid of these people because, even though I am not a slave, I am beneath them. I have to talk to them, and some of them are arrogant and cruel, but, Leo, you are there with me, standing quietly behind me or speaking to them in your charming way, making them laugh or think. Leo—I know this is only a dream, but it seems so real to me, with your hands on my shoulders, knowing how frightened I am: yet you love me and—somehow you're helping me, like you are now—and, my love, if this dream helped me to remember you as you really are, and to trust in the gods, and to not be overcome with despair, then what difference if it is only a dream? For it is true anyway: you are helping me, through our little son, more than any dream...."

She stops then, her lips pressed against his forehead. He raises his face to hers, and they kiss each other's tears and cradle each other's faces. Then they lie quietly and sleep again, as the air lightens with a new dawn.

Eight

Beginning this journal approximately two weeks after the fall of Western civilization, for all the usual reasons: posterity, the edification of our descendants, etc. etc. Actually, there would seem to me to be a certain amount of futility connected with the project, given the quality of the holders of the gene pool who have survived. At least, those into whom I have run. Oh, to be sure, there are the usual salt of the earth types, and others rushing heroically into the breach. But intellect and refinement? As far as I can ascertain, these qualities have not been conducive to survival.

Not that this will be any kind of true literary endeavor. I also recognize that another, if not the main reason, why I am doing this is for its therapeutic effect on my own mental and emotional health. Communing with myself and all that. Paper is one thing not in short supply, for now. There are reams of it everywhere. Even that is beside the point: I'm sure I'll be dead before I complete this journal, no matter how long-winded the entries. No room for aging professors of history in this new age, I'm afraid.

I'm sure there is ample evidence for my hypothetical reader of the causes of the present collapse. These can undoubtedly be traced back to the dawn of time, but such a task is obviously not my responsibility, at this time, anyway. The years I spent doing just that in my classes and published work would appear to have come to naught, in any case, utterly unheeded as it all was. Of course there was a nagging voice assuring me of this all along, and yet the ego will have its way.

To make a very long story very short, things just got worse. Beginning with the election of the Great Deceiver, this country joined with the world on a journey of self-delusion and escapism that would have done Nero proud. With the final sequence of inflation, bad credit indefinitely extended, political instability, and the exponential proliferation of environmental catastrophe, all these systems were so interlinked that the result became inevitable.

Chaos reigns, in the truest sense. By this I don't mean unbridled destruction, rather unpredictability. The impact of the loss of all mass communication is primary, and astounding. In fact, I believe I detect within myself a feeling of grief at this loss, distinct from other sources. Money is another bewildering vacancy. It has become worthless, replaced by barter or force, although some are neurotically still clinging to it and attempting to wrest some meaning from it. Naturally, food is very unpredictable—when, where and what. I currently possess mostly canned goods, but yesterday the whole building was treated to delicious fresh-baked bread, cooked in some interesting fire-powered makeshift oven that someone devised.

People are traveling around, with and without destinations. Reports from other places vary from nuclear holocaust to utopia.

There are about two dozen of us in this building.

I have lost all of my

October 3

Interrupted yesterday by news of terrorist gangs proliferating in the area. The population of the building met in the basement and debated heatedly between staying and barricading, dispersing, and moving as a group to another place. I am indifferent. It seems to me the odds of being harmed are the same regardless.

Indifferent as well today to this project. Information about real events is so garbled it is pointless to record it. If, on the other hand, I record the interactions and minutiae in this building, it resembles some ludicrous movie: it's all been done before (character studies, personal metamorphosis, power struggles, heroism and breakdowns, and the like).

As for the contents of my own mind, these are too banal for words. I am no Anne Frank, and I'm sure the last things the world would want to read are the mutterings and obsessions of a bitter sixty-year-old man who began ossifying long before this event occurred. All reactions thoroughly predictable.

I will note that I have detected a sensation within myself of relief. It was a while before I realized this, always encountering the obstacle of the fact that I was a tenured professor (even though I had not been paid for two months prior to the bombing) and therefore had a pathetically symbiotic relationship with my mother the university, comforts to look forward to in old age, etc., in return for absolutely minimal effort. I long thought the seething resentments I had cultivated over a span of thirty years for that same monstrous institution, had just boiled dry; but I suppose in an indirect way, that they are the source of this relief. I didn't have to throw it all away, it was taken, so I escaped with honor in a way.

October 9

Two of our number are missing. Unlikely that anything except harm would have caused this, given their natures. We have grown close, those of us here, in our own ways, and there is a keeping track of each other, like ants touching feelers and shedding pheromones wherever they go. In a way of course this is touching, and in a way it's just pathetic.

One of our number is becoming sickly. I believe that some others besides myself suspect radiation or some other nonreversible chemical effect, but nothing is being said.

My role as the detached intellectual has become accepted, in the way group dynamics tend to form. I am not particularly aware of any repressed yearning within myself to change this. I can't get away from viewing things this way, of seeing how stereotypical almost any such "warming" behavior would be. Not to mention the ever-present futility.

I am actually quite comfortable in my little room. It is an average little studio. I am reminded of my student days. There is a nice bay window with a large ledge. I sleep there on a cot, with pillows and blankets, and look up into the stars.

October 14

Rumors seem to be consolidating around the area to the west of here as being the place to go. Relatively uncontaminated. Of course all the talk about energy centers and new beginnings is so much New Age suggestion, but what people believe is what they seem to make real, in a way, so if they think the locale is special, then why rob them of the illusion, especially if they then can find the heart to act on their hope. Would that I could find such faith. This is not to attempt to distance myself from "the masses" as if I'm somehow too sophisticated for faith. I have sought such a thing, at times passionately when I was younger, but something in me seems to just reject all of the vast array of possible "paths" available.

An odd development, irrelevant to everything—there is a young woman in our little group, Diane by name, who I have recently gotten the distinct impression has formed some sort of attachment to me. It's rather difficult to articulate my reaction to this, especially since it's only an impression. She seems to end up sitting beside me in our little basement meetings, I seem to catch her eyes on me.... Perhaps I am sensitive (or overly so) to this kind of phenomenon because of my various experiences of it with my female students over the years. Of course I suppose it's natural on her part to seek a father figure, given the situation.

October 17

Trouble in paradise...after dying down a bit, there are once again some heated opinions being expressed about relocation. Things are heating up around here in that many of the displaced people have departed, leaving only those who are entrenched such as ourselves, the criminals, and the "pioneers" who are breaking up the concrete and more or less starting small farms here in the city. The city is already almost unrecognizable, really transforming before our eyes. It is hard to avoid some feeling for the new growth arising from the old destruction, even though I would hardly wax poetic about it as some do.

I doubt that I would leave. The thought of dressing up for a long winter's foot-journey to an uncertain destination seems ludicrous. There are a couple of others who are simply unfit for such an undertaking: I could remain with them, presumably until we starve or are killed. With the insidious poisons unleashed all around us by the Breakdown, I doubt it really matters anyway.

The younger ones are all up for it, of course, Diane included. And they are probably right in this: their hope and courage well might see them through. Diane

Later

Speak of the devil, figuratively speaking of course: she just paid me a visit. My suspicious are borne out: one thing I'll say for myself is that I know that look in a woman's eyes when I see it. And Diane is not skilled at dissembling, nor do I think she ever will be, given her nature.

And what is that nature, might my reader ask, coming awake with the first interesting development in this entire tedious undertaking. Well, reader, you can go back to sleep, not because Diane herself isn't worth the interest, but because nothing will come of it anyway.

Not that I could explain that nature, but I will try to, having brought it up. If I sound a bit addled, let me explain that she is in her early 20s and has soft blond ringletted hair, the kind of blond that's streaked with brown. Yet her personality is as warm and giddy as the darkest señorita's. And it would be unfair as well as inaccurate to omit the fact that she possesses an absolutely exquisite beauty of the china-doll variety. Imagine a china doll happiest in blue jeans, and there you have her.

So of course I'm aware of a normal response to her on my part. This doesn't negate the fact that the situation is ridiculous. One more item: I know that a couple of the fellows in our little group would willingly forfeit the proverbial right arm for sex with her, and she seems to be sustaining perfectly normal friendships with the half dozen people in her age group who I suppose consider themselves the most "enlightened," or at least normal. Granted, I'm not a *hideous* old man, still it disturbs me that she should have singled me out in this way. The odd thing is that she seems self-sufficient and energetic enough, so why would she emphasize this need for a father figure?

Anyway, she came in and at first we made small talk, and she sort of wandered and looked around (I've salvaged a few interesting things from the rubble). She has a way about her of appearing confident and insecure simultaneously, sort of like a yearling cat. Nothing neurotic, rather charming and fresh, at least to me. Feminists would consider her too kittenish, traditionalists too brazen.

Anyway *again* (I am quite aware of my preoccupied rambling, thank you), finally she got around to trying to talk me into committing to coming along. We went back and forth once again over the pros and cons, on and on.

If she were a student, I would say she was after nothing more insidious than to be sure she was on my good side, since she really does not have the mind for facts; or else the typical brief infatuation. But still I can hardly see a motive for her interest in me. I could sense my depression and my feelings of futility about the future like a shield around me as I encounter her encouragements and questioning. Truly the last thing I need is to be led off on some futile chase across the country by a pair of beautiful eyes, and of that I am certain.

October 18

They will leave under cover of pre-dawn darkness tomorrow.

The light is dying now. I may be a dried out, rigid old fool, but I am reasonably aware of my feelings, counter to stereotype, and I will admit here a mingling of griefs, both at the loss of people I could regard as friends, and a more latent one that Diane didn't return for another shot at persuading me. There, I've admitted it. Not that it would have mattered anyway.

I am considering suicide, at this point only as a last resort. If unhappiness were the reason, I would have done it many years ago: primarily now my concern is food and water. Without the able-bodied and energetic here any longer, I am not certain how long I will have the heart to scavenge by myself. Winter is here. Why prolong the agony?

October 21

Much has changed. We are huddled under a bridge for the night, and I am writing by strong moonlight. The "we" refers to Diane and myself.

Apparently, on the night of my last entry, our building threw a very small but vocal going-away celebration. Normally we kept our building façade obscured and closed to prevent gangs from knowing it was occupied, but the festivities on that night apparently attracted the notice of one gang that was coincidentally passing through. I was in my room, and I heard the all-too-familiar sounds of gunfire, screams, shouts, and random miscellaneous violence. According to Diane, there was resistance from some of our group, fighting, and somehow a fire broke out. With no water to spare, it spread rapidly.

After ascertaining what was happening, after the first flood of adrenaline had sent me around my little room collecting my things, after lightning-quick montages and voices in my mind rehearsed the various probably outcomes of this, I reverted to a plan I had devised long ago: I sat down and began taking the câche of pills I had secreted.

My room was on an upper story of the building. I heard voices, laughter and door-slammings approaching me. I lay down in my nook. I wondered if they just would take my things, or if they were gratuitously violent.

Then I heard knocking, and Diane's voice. I let her in, and she began begging me to come with her and some of the others, to try to get out. We argued: finally I told her the deed was done. To my amazement she began punching me in the stomach, and yelling for me to throw them up, which I almost did. Finally I got her hands and stopped her, and shouted at her quite angrily to leave. Why won't you leave me alone, I asked her over and over, and to my further amazement I began to cry. She did too, and smoke began coming in, and the voices were getting closer. For the last few seconds, we just stood there, stalemated, hurt and holding each other.

They raped her, two of them, and hit me a few times just to get me out of the way. I vomited then, and since once I begin I have to empty, I lost all the pills. They cleaned out my room, trashing what they couldn't use, and left us on the floor.

By the time we crept out of the building, avoiding the area

where we could hear their voices settling in for a good night's brawl with our carefully hoarded provisions (I guess they put the fire out), several hours had passed. Even if the others had been waiting for us, we had no idea where, and could hardly have gone shouting through the streets

October 27

Amazingly, we are doing a little better now. It seems too good to be true that we are surviving out here as well as we are. It is cold but not as cold as it could be, and will be all too soon, unless the climate has indeed warmed due to the recent bombings, volcanic eruptions and all that crap. Global warming.

On the other hand, surviving seems easier than I imagined it would be. One foot in front of the other, keep your things together, keep alert. We have my treasured hoard of butane lighters which I keep wrapped in plastic and secreted away, bringing one out every once in a while as a good trade; tonight we actually have a fire going. We have sleeping bags and a blanket, a container of drinking water, some food and a pot. She's wearing my clothes and we have a change apiece. We don't have proper packs though, and it's amazing how bothersome and heavy it is lugging these few pitiful things around all the time just slung over our shoulders.

I am also amazed (I'm aware suddenly of how often I seem to be using that word, but it fits) by how much better we feel out of the city. There is scarcely a place untouched by ruin, but the constant pressure of fear in the city is gone. This may be fallacious because we could be attacked just as effectively out here, but we both feel it. It has also helped morale not to encounter quite the density of dead bodies and garbage out here as in the city. Night before last we drowned our horror in alcohol-induced hilarity, but the regret the next morning was intense: that method of coping has been quietly abandoned.

Today we passed through a park that I was familiar with

from before the End, and suddenly I felt completely weak, actually on the point of collapse. I sat down on a bench, my heart pounding, trembling. There was no pain—all I could think of was that I was having a breakdown or stroke or something, and I was terrified. She asked me what was wrong and I tried to explain. My voice trembled, I couldn't get my words together and I felt twenty years older. I was terribly embarrassed—here she was, she was the one who'd been assaulted and now she was stuck with a doddering old man to drag along.

She made a remarkably intuitive connection and asked me if it was seeing the park and remembering it from before, and suddenly I was simply overwhelmed with emotion, the most powerful I have ever experienced, bar none, and began crying with huge sobs, completely forgetting myself. Images from my childhood passed before my eyes so vividly I was actually frightened: they were mixed with images from all the rest of my life before the End. Was it her murmuring in my ear, "Go ahead, go ahead," that made me surrender to those images, or would I have had no choice anyway? I don't know.

In a way of course I have felt better since then, more energy, unbelievably a little more optimism. But I'm also more uncomfortable, feel vulnerable all the time: I thought emotional release was supposed to make you feel more secure.

The fire is dying and it's time for us to sleep.

October 29

I can see this thing is going to be pretty worthless. I'm not including much description of what we see around us or what we hear of the rest of the country. More contradictions: on the one hand everything is completely changed; there's no pulling in somewhere to buy what we need or to listen to the news. Yet on the other hand, the ground and trees and many buildings are still here, we do come across all the familiar detritus: toothpaste and candy bars and tires. Also, most of the people we encounter are still just people. Most are exceedingly nice. We have traded some things, and given or been given others. I cried again, although quietly and to myself (of course Diane knew) when we were invited yesterday to sit at some folks' fire to eat. I don't know what kind of meat they were roasting, and the greens were bitter, but I've never tasted a meal so good.

The irony is not lost on me that whereas before I had all the time in the world but little to write about, now, when my writing time is limited, there is so much to say. Should I write about Diane? I don't really know yet what to say about her. Should I write about how I feel like I'm going through a second adolescence or something, with all its unpredictability and intensity? Should I write about my world view or Philosophy of Life, which right now is almost totally chaotic, with old elements swimming around uneasily with the new? It all is truly intensified by the fact that I can't hold onto any of it: we could literally die at any moment.

I think there is one important element, though, that I should mention: each time my thoughts begin to hunker down into their old rut of futility, there is some kind of resistance. Nothing so naive as a Scrooge-like overnight change of heart or anything: I still believe things are rotten and it's best not to hope for too much. But what started as oral self-censorship because I know it saddens her when I speak like that, seems to have sunk in somehow, and now I censor or rather divert my own thoughts almost habitually, to at least keep an open mind, to at least not completely disregard and ignore the good things that seem to regularly come our way: the indescribable feeling of warmth when the sun is out and my feet and fingers and face thaw and I feel a surge of energy, the way some part of me that I still quite deliberately avoid really encountering dares to hope that I will live to spend another day looking into her eyes, making her laugh, feeling astoundingly protective of her (without any basis in reality, of course)! I've realized that all these years I was wrong about what I construed as the self-confident, beautiful nymphet who only feigns sweetness and vulnerability. Diane, at least, is the real thing. Thank God all she seems to require for reassurance is my presence, because I certainly feel I have little else to offer.

October 31—Halloween!
(if I've kept track accurately)

The hardest part was at the beginning, I see now. We are in such a routine that I almost feel I could go on like this indefinitely. Not that we don't engage in verbal drooling over images of a warm bed and hot running water (I will set up a shrine to Hot Running Water if I ever get out of this) and movies and hopping in the car for an errand. We had a hilarious good laugh (one of many) over a shared elaborate and detailed fantasy about eating out, from fast food to expensive: just going into a restaurant and having anything we wanted, and as much.

That aside, many of my aches have moderated and my entire mental and physical being is less weary and more certain. This is again a natural and even predictable development: it's predictability, however, does not mitigate its impact. The effect on Diane has been less severe, since she was healthy and flexible to begin with.

I still don't feel adequate to put in words what I feel about her. My relationships with women, whether intimate or less so, have been limited, my marriage a Victorian anachronism, so I know that puts a spotlight on this one. But I can't accept that what we have is common, even less that she is. We are not lovers, but I feel closer to her than to anyone I've shared a bed with. Part of me could begin writing about her and never stop, but part of me wants to say nothing to anyone, wants to keep her, and us, completely to myself. It *is* very much like a butterfly resting on the palm of my hand, and I am frozen, afraid of any movement.

How could I express all that passes between us without sounding mundane and predictable? How can I if I don't understand it myself? How can I separate fact from my fantasy?

More pertinent, what place has all this in a journal of the end of a civilization?

November 2

She began menstruating today, allying residual fears from the assault.

I am in love with her, I might as well face it. Of course she knows it, because she loved me first.

Of course I desire her too, but that is a slightly different issue. I hardly dare even fantasize about her, although naturally her face floats before me when I masturbate (yes, time must be made for such things even on the road at the end of the world).

Her father was a powerful, cold man, and molested her regularly when she was a teen. She adored (adores?) him and craved his attention and approval, and was a semi-willing participant. Now she views herself as "just a whore," although she has never been promiscuous.

I am at a loss as to how to deal with this, so I don't. The topic was addressed in a slew of books just before the End. There seemed to be an epidemic of it then, or at least its exposure. So the world hardly needs my analysis. Especially since I don't know her father. But I have certainly been thinking about it, trying to understand, and to then understand her better and myself better, and where to go from there. She doesn't want to talk about it, and I don't know whether that's best, or if she *should* just put it behind her. But I know it still hurts her whatever she says, I can actually physically feel it in my heart, a physical sensation in my chest and in my throat.

Am I supposed to sustain an ideal Platonic friendship with her, regardless of what we both want, in order to prove that love doesn't have to be sexual? *Does* she want me, or is that desire entwined with that other issue, and only a reflexive, surface phenomenon? Is it really my responsibility to play the role of "good father" in his place? I have asked myself a hundred questions, and I haven't any answers.

November 12

We've been heading pretty much due west since we began, following the leads of food and shelter to move us in specific directions along the way. Today for the first time we met up with another couple who are heading to a place where we think we would like to go. We spent some time together and consequently have joined paths: it is a few days' distance from here.

Never given to sustained, intimate friendships of any kind, it is amazing to me how easy it has been to relate to Tom and Sarah. They just are so natural, and that is I guess the way Diane and I are, or are moving toward, or trying to.

It has been interesting to me to see them interact: although close in age, Tom is exuberant and Sarah is more sedate, so in an odd way there seems to me to be a maternal quality in the way she is to him. Undoubtedly though I am picking this up because of my preoccupation. As I mentally examine other couples I have known, I automatically seek out demonstrations of that dynamic—comparing, analyzing. What is its part in relationships?

It is apparently a very large house we're heading toward, in operation since before the Breakdown. They say the emphasis is on freedom and responsibility; grand words indeed, I know, but from what they describe, meant in a true sense, like anarchy. No rules, no authorities, no excuses. It was a combination of this description with who Tom and Sarah are, rather than the description alone, though, that has induced us to give it a shot.

It is another matter of surprise to me, how Diane and I are received by others. We introduce ourselves as friends, but there have been no reactions I could detect of ridicule or judgment, among any of the people we've met. I guess this is due, a great deal anyway, to the fact that people are so preoccupied with survival, and also to the general feeling of camaraderie in crisis, so that many ideological divisions are suspended or have fallen by the wayside.

November 20

We hope to reach our destination tomorrow.

It has been extraordinarily moving to be with these people the past few days. Last night around our fire, the four of us actually talked about Diane and myself. Things were said and unsaid, but the overall feeling was so accepting, so open and loving, it was almost like a benediction in a way. I simply know that whatever we decide about each other will be accepted by them. There was some "New Age" talk about other lives and such, but they are not fanatic and their general gist is that the conscious self and inner self (or unconscious?) must work together, via conscious beliefs and decisions working with impulses and intuition, desire and feeling.

Sarah and Diane spend a lot of time together, and Tom and I have as well. I am grateful for this. Diane needs someone like Sarah, and god help me I can sure use Tom's friendship and advice, since I have never felt more vulnerable, confused and chaotic. Yet, there is an exhilaration in my life that I never dreamed possible. They have taught us both an exceedingly simple "centering device," sitting and breathing and focusing, that always quickly restores calm to me. And on and on, many little insights and such, most of which I don't accept outright, but I do listen and I have an open mind toward them. Time will tell. Much of what they say seems to "feel" right anyway.

Just one interesting detail, Sarah mentioned a strong bond between Diane and myself in a life in medieval Europe, and we had to laugh because medieval history is my specialty, and Diane had previously mentioned a recurrent, lifelong fantasy of hers in which she is a nun in an old European convent.

Of course Diane is like a sponge when it comes to these things, the problem is she has trouble discriminating and selecting what she is going to keep in terms of beliefs.

November 22

I hardly know where to begin today. I am sitting in a spare, beautiful room in a house that must contain fifty different living spaces. It is a marvelous place and Diane and I are going to remain at least for some time.

I hesitate to relate what happened between us last night, in respect for our privacy. But I do want to, I feel a real yearning to describe at least part of an experience that has so profoundly affected me.

We arrived here late yesterday, and when it came time to sleep, I felt she might like some privacy, her own room, after having been thrown together with me for almost a month. So I said as much to her. I'll never forget the sight of her standing in the dark hall. She was wearing long, simple white nightclothes and was wrapped in a heavy shawl. We had bathed and she looked fresher and more beautiful than ever. When I made my suggestion her face just fell, and she asked me didn't I want to keep sleeping together? And the hurt and the yearning, not as much sexual but so deep...

So we climbed into bed and I blew out the lamp. You can't imagine the sensual explosion of fresh clothes, clean bodies and a warm, soft bed after a month on the road. Temptation had not really been thrust upon us when we were exhausted, reeking, and exposed to the elements. Now however I didn't know how she expected me to behave, with her so soft and warm beside me.

This was compounded by the fact that as soon as she had climbed in she had turned her back to me and curled up as if to sleep, not shrinking from me but conveying some message, I knew. I knew she was afraid. I was irritated at first, and considered turning my back myself, just disassociating completely. Upon reflection, a process that would have taken me days before the Breakdown had I bothered at all but that now took me only minutes, I realized that I was afraid too: I didn't want to lose her either by doing the wrong thing or doing nothing at all. I felt that there were many ways to lose Diane.

I turned toward her, close but not crowding. Ironically, the physical, sexual aspects of being with a woman have never caused me any discomfort: it is the emotional realm in which I have never been completely at ease. Now that I had decided that she must desire me beneath her fear (if she didn't, it was time that we confronted the issue before it ranged into the area of poor health), I began to be suffused with the love I felt for her, and began opening to all that it encompassed. In a moment that stretched into forever, that I saw myself rehearsing uncounted times before I actually moved, I touched her hair, began very slowly, slowly stroking it, breathing into it, our first sexual moment.

She lay frozen, and my throat became choked, the lump hurting so that it was almost unbearable, because I knew as plainly as my name all the things she was feeling. After a few minutes I asked her simply if she wanted me to stop. From deep down in her pillow, there was a world of feeling in the muffled "No." I began to touch her back and her arm through the nightclothes. I began to experience an odd feeling that I can only call detachment, combined with a strange knowing, beyond the sexual knowing with which I was familiar. It was almost as if some other, latent part of my personality began rising to the surface. This is venturing into the realm of the indescribable, or of descriptions that sound too absurd or strange to convey their true meaning.

Suddenly she turned to me and pressed her lips to mine, and I think I have never felt such amazement since my first kiss several hundred years ago. I was flooded with, it seemed, all the memories of looking at those lips, consciously and half consciously wanting them for some time now. At the same time I was amazed at something totally unexpected: she actually had very little idea of what she was doing at the deeper level: her motions were all flash and surface. Again this harks back to my previous conviction that the girls of her age and generation were de facto sexual experts. I tasted her tears and felt her eagerness, desperation actually. Suddenly I was aware that this was how her father had "trained" her, to be lascivious, to enact the cardboard cutout performances of pornography, all for the camera, and her other young, passionate lovers had none of them yet discovered the incredible escalation of pleasure and feeling that comes from really focusing and taking one's time.

I slowed her down, feeling some amusement. Slowly, slowly I spent a world of time on her mouth and face, felt her surprise, felt her respond and fall in with my pace. Meanwhile, this strange other self of mine sensed when she detached into performance, became "another self" of hers, in a way, and when it was the real Diane; what was the surface, and what was the soul.

On we went into the night, inch by precious inch. Then I touched her in a way I knew immediately her father had, and she flinched and tightened, and then was simply "not there," and responded only reflexively. I gently disengaged and relit the lamp. It's hard for me to remember, let alone describe, the next interval of time. We talked, and I felt this "other self" very strongly in me, and acquiesced to "his" guidance to a great extent, saying and doing and knowing things I wouldn't have ordinarily, things that pushed her, pushed both of us, right up to the issue instead of trying to "heal" it right away. A knife lancing a boil, rather than soaking it in hot bandages for days.

In other words, we enacted some things spontaneously, to the point of her finally, helplessly releasing herself to her rage and beating on me with her fists, exhausting herself into tears and then understanding, and on and on. Then the ghosts were gone, at least for the time being, and with the lamp still burning very low, I took her on my lap and, seeing each others' eyes and faces very clearly, we made love with a stillness and intensity that neither of us had ever dreamed possible.

I don't know what will become of us. Surely it would be natural for her to fall in love someday with someone her own age, as it would for me! Yet we "were one" for a time last night, and I know for a fact that we will never be completely out of each others' hearts. That is worth more than the number of days we end up spending or not spending together.

December 2

This will be my last entry for a while. I am involved in various activities, working and learning with Tom, but that is not the reason. The situation is simply that I'm undergoing such changes in the ways that I think that it's difficult to know exactly what I think may or may not be happening, the meanings behind things, that is. There are some things I am trying out, ways to manipulate reality, ways to interpret it, understand it, that have penetrated to the foundations of, remarkably enough, who I think I am. Or it might be the other way around; in fact that seems strangely, exactly so. Also part of it is that so much of this feels so private, and so much happens so quickly, and in clusters of events or meanings.

The reader is aware of my attitude toward all the latest trends—I simply must do more sifting, let some of these experiences sink in, or fade away. I don't know if I'm going to resume. It could be that I will divert the energy into teaching or a different kind of writing.

Diane is radiant, a rose bursting into bloom on the first long, warm spring day. Our days' activities are diverse and usually separate, but she still sleeps with me a part of the time, and gives me long, long kisses in the late afternoon.

Nine

"Susan, sit still for mother now, you know what we agreed on," says Susan's mother, holding her daughter's hands fast in her lap. But Susan is no vase of flowers, to be arranged and left; she is a big, strapping girl, and she definitely does not want to sit still. Grunting and sending reproachful glances at her mother, she continues to struggle.

"Mrs. Halvorsam, how nice to see you," says the doctor coming into the waiting room.

"Oh, hello doctor, I'm so glad you were in. She's..." begins the mother tiredly.

"And Susan, how are you today?"

Susan has stopped struggling and has quieted her motion. She eyes the doctor blankly.

"Still don't like to come see your old friend, do you? You must get over this, you're—what, seventeen now?" he directs this last at the mother, who confirms it with a long-suffering smile. "Big girls aren't afraid of the doctor, now are they?"

"Oh, it's not that she minds coming here so much, doctor,

140

see how good she is for you? No, it's me she fights, day and night; she's as bad as ever, doctor, and she's getting so strong, so—willful, I don't know what I'm going to do with her. And I'm sorry to say this about my own daughter, but her temper is absolutely vile. How can she get so upset about things, be so moody, when she's not...normal, doesn't understand anything that's going on, you know? Why can't she just be a good girl and do her sewing and live quiet with me?"

"Well, Mrs. Halvorsam, she may not understand things, but she has feelings," the doctor explains patiently, sitting and regarding Susan quietly. "I've explained all that to you."

"Yes, yes, I know she has feelings," says Mrs. Halvorsam impatiently and a little shortly. "But I thought youthful rebellion was due to the child disagreeing with the parents, and how can she disagree with me when there's nothing to disagree about? She doesn't understand enough to disagree about anything! We lead the same life, and I'm happy, or at least contented—why can't she be? Is it so much to ask for her to taste her food and feel the clothes on her back and the warmth of the hearth and show a little gratitude along with all that other vile, headstrong behavior of hers?" she implores the doctor, close to tears of frustration.

"Now, now, Mrs. Halvorsam, I know you're upset now and I don't want to upset you further, but I have made various suggestions—"

"Oh, of course you have," she replies, rising in anger. "Let this innocent babe wander down into the village, anywhere and anytime she wants, consort with whom she wants—"

"Mrs. Halvorsam, school is hardly wander-"

"I know, I know," she admits, fingers pinching the skin between her brows. "Even aside from that, though, I can imagine how frantic she would be coming home from all that fraternizing every day, and you can't, you simply can't guarantee that she wouldn't be—wouldn't be—"

"No, no guarantees," sighs the doctor, but he and Susan are staring intently at each other. "Raped" floats on the air between the three of them and then slinks through a crack in the floor. "Still, I wish you'd consider it. I'm more and more certain that Susan's problem lies only in the higher reasoning processes. I'm convinced that with care and patience she can be trained, as any child can, as you have done with her already and can see for yourself."

"I agree, I agree, but sometimes I think you don't understand that Susan doesn't want to be trained; a lot of the time she disregards what she knows in the rush, this headlong compulsion to have her own way." Mrs. Halvorsam sniffs and gathers herself to leave. She could never have articulated it even to herself, but something in the way they are regarding each other has made her feel excluded. She doesn't want to know about it though.

"She needs activity and variation just as any other adolescent does. As any human being does," the doctor says, the last very quietly.

"What?"

"Oh, nothing. An hour then?"

"Yes. I'll be at the market and then at the vicar's. Thank you so much, Doctor. I don't know what I would have done without you. God bless Freud or whoever invented this hypnosis, I don't know what people did before it..."

Susan stalks into the examining room like a wary panther, giving every appearance of imminent struggle and flight. The doctor follows, shutting the door behind him. He turns to face her. She eyes the door, listening. "Yes, she's gone," he says quietly, and the tiniest hint of a smile winks out from the fuzzy gray fibers of his beard.

Suddenly Susan's face is suffused with the most radiant smile. Practically bursting, she runs up to him and flings herself upon him, leaping up to wrap her legs around, too. It is an extraordinarily incongruous sight, the long, elegantly sinewy white things jutting out from the properly-waistcoated waist like wings. He grasps her buttocks to sustain her weight as she smothers his face in kisses.

"There's my girl, but you know you're getting too hefty

for this, and I'm getting too old," he says as he steps heavily to the examining table and sets her down on it with a thump. She keeps holding him, kissing him, urgency reflecting out of her dark, searching eyes and suddenly serious face, slowing her. "There, there, it'll be all right soon," he murmurs kindly, and reaching up, strokes her hair and face. "Now, let's see what we have here..."

"There you are," says the doctor as a younger, blond man enters the office.

"Yes, delayed a bit," he replies, removing hat and coat and coming toward the table. He hesitates a moment before he reaches it, then whistles through his teeth. "Jeez, this is the one you were telling me about, isn't it?"

"Yes."

"Sorry, she. What's her name? Susan?"

"Yes."

He gingerly takes another step. "Do you think she would mind if I came closer?"

"Geoffrey."

"Sorry again."

"I mean she's right here for Chrissakes. You'd ask a dog directly, wouldn't you, even knowing it doesn't understand the words?"

"All right, I said I was sorry." His manner is genuine. "Susan, do you mind if I come closer?"

Susan lies on the examining table, the lamp shining whitely on her perfect alabaster skin. She is calm now, and gazes down at the older man with an expression still quite serious, but laced with love and a smile. She glances at Geoffrey, a little curious, but it's a half-asleep, dream curiosity. She re-locks her eyes with those of the doctor and moves a shoulder with her smile, shyly.

The doctor glances at Geoffrey and Geoffrey comes closer. Geoffrey looks with great interest at the lovely body, the perfection and sweetness of the curves, the thighs parted easily, knees dangling down on either side of the doctor. His nostrils move a little as her scent passes into them. He watches the doctor's hand gently stroking her belly, and feels an erection begin to build.

"Je—sus, you weren't exaggerating, Frank. She's ...incredible."

"Mmm," Frank the doctor replies. It is a distant "mmm." It sounds like it originated in the same half-asleep, dream realm as Susan's glance at Geoffrey.

"Have you already—?" asks Geoffrey.

"Yes."

"So she..." and he trails off, slight embarrassment making him uncertain as to how to approach his question. "You know, she really doesn't look..."

"I know. It *is* mild, but it's provoked by a quite volatile temperament." The doctor doesn't try to disguise his fondness as he says this. Susan's smile broadens momentarily. Geoffrey suddenly thinks of a lagoon, and lost boys, and a beautiful young girl who didn't want to grow up, who wanted to fly. He has some occasional imagination, this young man.

"I'm afraid her mother's right," Frank continues slowly. "Most of her problem is an unwillingness to learn." Long pause. "At least to learn what her mother wants to teach her," he mutters.

A beat. "Well thank God for that," Geoffrey breathes. He looks at the older man surreptitiously, waiting for him to give in and smile. He is rewarded, and they share a quiet laugh. Susan smiles again, sitting up, but listening as we listen to music, construing meaning from an essentially alien language.

"Susan, this is Geoffrey, another doctor, a friend. I'm teaching him. We were laughing because we're happy that you think for yourself, and about how you and I fooled your mother."

Susan laughs now, relieved to understand. Proud. She kisses him on the cheek, then glances at Geoffrey and turns slightly away, a little subdued.

"What, teaching her modesty too?"

"No, no, that's natural. It's just it has nothing to do with artificial sexual shame for her." His hand hovers over her arm and side.

"So does she do...does she understand..." Geoffrey tries again to ask, his tone low and significant.

"Pretty damned near everything," Frank interrupts in the same tone. "God help me, we've done it all," he sighs, and Geoffrey sees and hears the comic, bewildered rue. "It could be I'll burn in hell for it—"

"No, no, surely not," Geoffrey says soothingly, doubtfully, patting the older man's back. "Believe me, I see it the way you do, I think you're doing her a service. Sorry. You know what I mean. I mean from the way you described it..."

"I swear to God that's how it happened. Two years ago, making her fifteen, her mother brings her in here, the both of them half-hysterical. She's never been in a doctor's office, furious at her mother, furious at the world. I get the mother out, somehow get Susan calmed a little. I start to talk to her, start to examine her. She's pinning me with these eyes, well, you can see them. I swear to God, she fell in love with me at first sight." The doctor turns to Geoffrey, awe and defiance in his voice.

"Now I know that's common, I know what you're going to say. I handled her with complete professionalism. She had a UTI, I did a pelvic. The poor creature lay there looking at me, and she's drenched, fully aroused.... Turns out the mother burned her fingers for masturbating when she was a child so she doesn't, and Geoffrey, she is such a passionate creature." Geoffrey carefully doesn't react when his friend is momentarily overwhelmed and holds Susan close. Geoffrey looks at her face, her eyes closed in quiet happiness.

"Suddenly I knew, I knew, that she thought she had been brought to me to alleviate her sexual need. She was just lying there, so grateful, needing so much, waiting...for...so I...couldn't help it. I just placed my thumb on her clitoris and held it there, and looked into those eyes, and she was so beautiful...so accepting...she looked like a goddess..."

Geoffrey looks with fascination at the two of them, almost nose to nose. Susan is listening to a symphony. He's never seen anything like it.

"It was all over in a couple of minutes. I suppose it would almost have been excusable if I'd just stopped there, but, well, then she began...to kiss me..." and Susan begins to smilingly kiss him, lightly, delicately, like a child would kiss a butterfly.

"And you got her to hide it from her mother, from...everybody?"

"Yes, although I might easily have failed at that, for all I knew, it's not like I plotted it beforehand. I was completely knocked off my feet. Thirty-two years of practice down the drain, potentially, including my share of hot-blooded young women successfully resisted to, thank you, to be brought down in the end by a retarded girl. But...she's never betrayed me." He turns to the girl.

"Susan, Geoffrey is going to work with me. I'm getting old, and he'll replace me when I retire."

Susan is very still, her smile ghostly. Suddenly, without looking at Geoffrey she pushes him in the chest, and inclines her head toward Frank again, briefly pressing her face into his neck. Geoffrey feels himself blush faintly as he understands what she understands.

But she doesn't look up at Frank. She looks away and down into a sudden chasm, and they see she can contemplate death.

Frank holds her very tenderly. "Of course, we hope by then your mother will let you go to school, or have friends of your own. And you will touch yourself, and love yourself again," he murmurs the last sternly, and she nods with a hard-won acquiescence. "And you won't need to come here to see the doctor," he says into her hair, his voice kind of fading.

Geoffrey cannot get over his amazement at this relationship. Yet on the other hand, it seems eerily natural, too. Only one thing he does know at this point is that risk or not, if the day ever comes where Susan turns to him in her need, he hopes to be there, he plans to be there, to hold up his end of the bargain. At least once.

"Hell, maybe I'll even marry her," he mutters to himself. Thoughtfully, he places his hand on the center of her back, and she turns to look at him, from very far away.

Ten

Once upon a time there lived a beloved old king with his queen, in a fine castle in a prospering land. This was in the time before things became fixed, when fairies and giants and all manner of other creatures had largely disappeared, but could still be found occasionally. In this kingdom, there were races of animal-people dwelling in secluded pockets of old forest, generally in the mountainous regions. These races kept to separate ways and interests, and were largely known to humans through legend, although there were occasional glimpses and contacts between the two. The people might have been more curious about their mysterious neighbors, but truth to tell, the general drift of opinion was that the wolf-, bear-, and cat-people were a notch below humans in the order of things.

Nevertheless the kingdom was known favorably for its lack of strife, both between races and within the human population itself.

Nothing particular stood out in the reign of the king that would directly explain his success. Certainly he reflected the tolerance of his people, but he was not a terribly active king. He liked to settle disputes and was good at it, and his queen liked to plan for the crops and other events and was good at that. Everything else was also taken care of one way or another.

What the king and queen loved most of all was to ride. Not to hunt, for the queen had a distaste for it, and the king a positive aversion to causing needless pain to animals. Rather, they rode for the pleasure itself, and had a weakness for horses: breeding and racing and showing them. But also they simply rode, sometimes in the wild, sometimes from village to village greeting their people.

One day during this activity they passed into some very wild country. An animal-person, in one of its daydreams, stepped onto a trail in front of the queen's horse, and she was thrown down a steep, stony hillside to her death. It was a freak accident, but one which permitted her to depart while still in full vigor, the king's sage reassured him; a path chosen by many of the more adventuresome souls.

The king did take comfort from this, resonating as it did with what he privately felt about his wife's personality. He grieved for her, and after a few months he began to heal, to expand back into his former activities and gregarious, curious self.

At a feast one evening he met the Lady Rowena from a neighboring kingdom to the east. There were a great many people at the feast and it grew quite boisterous. Rowena drank a lot of burgundy and danced on the table in her long dress of deep maroon, her dark hair flinging about and her dark eyes glowing with unaccustomed pleasure, for hers was a hard-working people.

"Now that is a fine woman," said the king, a little dazed by the wine and all the excitement. His friends looked knowingly on.

They were married soon after, for Rowena saw much advantage to her people from an alliance with this splendid kingdom, and took little account of her own personal interests. She treated her husband with respect in all ways.

Rowena was a capable administrator, to say the least. She began to, as she put it, "Set the kingdom to rights." This quietly rankled many tempers, as most considered that the kingdom, although not terribly efficient or modern, prospered well enough as it was. But Rowena, unlike her predecessor, had little playful use for free time: what else was there to do with time but work? She knew how to push for things slowly and persistently, and outlasted her opponents, one by one. Because she was laboring on their behalf, people's resentment could find no focus nor real volition, and her plans met with a gradual success.

Several years passed. Rowena, knowing her duty, had carefully submitted to the king's pleasure each month for a week of nights during her fertile period. The king, an ardent man no less now than ever, had first approached his wife with awe, with a virile adoration. Shocked and frightened by his curious, somewhat demanding ways with her, although she did not know it, she had met them with strict control and a respectful, undermining coolness that wounded his feelings and self-esteem with a long, slow, salty erosion. It wasn't long before, under the queen's carefully arranged conditions, the king's flesh failed to respond to his own bidding more often than not. They remained childless.

This was unfortunate, and yet there was a greater peril facing the kingdom, a peril whose approach had been just as slow and inexorable. This was the strange behavior of the weather. The strangeness lay in the temperature, for winter had lengthened and summer had cooled, until finally came the year in which winter did not retreat at all, and snow lay on the ground well into summer. Who could explain such an unknown thing? Fortunately, the queen's new measures had resulted in somewhat increased supplies of goods and few starved. But these were an active, carefree people. First the carefully controlled extra work, and now the sullen skies and air, and the rationing, had dampened their spirits; their gratitude to her was uneasy.

But the queen, although a disciplined, controlled woman,

was not brittle nor hard. She listened, she relented more often, not missing the irony that now, of course, the need for hard work was self-evident. She fasted in her chamber for days, withdrawn into herself and her thoughts—all to no avail. The weather remained the same.

She redoubled her efforts. She brought in more specialists, even seers and magicians, although her private beliefs held no room for them normally. People from her native land were brought in to teach the people advanced smithing and sewing skills so that they would have something to trade for food.

The king was debilitated and rather debauched by now. His cavalier management attempts, eclipsed by his wife's, faded and ceased. Her contempt for him was now barely masked. Many a scullery girl or tender-hearted cook crept up the stairs to his chambers to offer comfort. Many were those who crept back down with their blouse fronts stiff with his tears, having found such comfort to be all that he was able to accept from them.

So beloved was he, however, that no word against him, nor, by extension, Rowena, was uttered without compassion.

One day the queen was listening to seers gathered from near and far. An old, old woman sat stonily before her. "My gift is fading," she said.

"That's not true, Auntie," said her attendant, embarrassed. To the queen: "She cured our village of a plague only last month."

"My gift does not stretch to such heights."

"That's not true, Auntie," said the girl. "She straightened the mind of our own princess in three weeks' time," she told the queen.

"I have never practiced my craft in a strange land," scowled the old woman at her niece, who was looking at the queen beseechingly.

Rowena sat for a moment, her cradled knuckles tapping her lips. "An unwilling seer is worse than none, I think," she said at last in a low voice, disappointed, for she liked the look of this tactless hag. She rose slowly and walked to the window, gazing out upon the grays and browns of the palace grounds. "You may go," she said, and the hag did not miss the deep sigh in her voice, although Rowena tried to minimize it.

The hag stared at her for a minute. "Leave us," she said to her niece, who did so with hopeful relief. Rowena turned to the old woman as she shook out her cloth and lay it on the table. "I promise nothing," she said.

"I thank you for trying," Rowena replied, seating herself wearily before her.

The hag handed her some marked stones. "Throw them," she said. "Quickly."

Rowena did so, heedless of where they landed on the brightly colored cloth. The hag stared down, but seemed to Rowena strangely unheeding of their positions. Several long moments passed.

"I was right, I can see nothing," the hag said suddenly. She began to gather the cloth but Rowena touched her arm.

"Please. I am strong enough to hear the truth, and I can bear it," she said in the time-honored manner.

The hag sat back. "Very well." She paused, looking into Rowena's eyes, then looked away. "Your marriage is childless," she stated.

Rowena took care not to reveal a reaction to this. "Yes."

"...although you are both fertile," continued the hag, still courteously looking down, although Rowena knew she didn't need to study the stones further.

"I wouldn't know, we've neither of us had children." Rowena's heart was sinking: was this to be just another hesitant pointing-out of the parallel she herself had seen before anyone? Silence stretched out. "We have followed all the various procedures quite carefully," she finally added.

Slowly the hag raised her eyes. "Let us not pretend. Surely you know the sadness lies not in the loins, but the heart, and there is no procedure for that."

Rowena's pride forbade her flinching, but she felt quite stung. "What has this to do with the winter, Auntie? Practically speaking," she asked, renewed control deepening her voice.

"Practically speaking...there is a man who walks at night. You must find him."

Rowena frowned. "Where?" she asked after a moment.

"In the forest."

Rowena set her mouth, and turned to look through the window once again. She didn't like the forest. "Tell me more."

"You must begin on your first fertile night, alone, taking very little. You must keep walking until you find the circle of red. Linger there, and he will come to you."

"Why cannot my husband go on this...quest?" When the hag didn't answer, Rowena turned to look at her, then lowered her eyes in shame. "Is there no other way?" she asked finally.

"The only other way lies right before your eyes, as you go about your daily activities, should you open them."

"Open my eyes to what?" Rowena asked rather sharply.

"To yourself, and then to all that is about you as a reflection thereof."

"I don't understand," Rowena said impatiently.

"That's why I suggested the woods."

"Very well, thank you for your help. You shall be paid as you leave." She turned to the window again, but heard the hag step up softly behind her.

"The solution for your kingdom shall be a great blessing for you too, milady. A land cannot thrive when its queen suffers so deeply."

Rowena felt tears. "Thank you," she said stiffly.

"Heed your dreams, child, and bless you," and she left.

The queen remained long at the window, and saw no more seers that day. Something had struck her about the old woman, and she warmed to the idea of going on this quest.

A journey alone, into the cold. If she never returned, if she were frozen or devoured, at least the people would know she had done her best. At one point, during the days that followed, in a cloud of darkness she wondered if that were what the land wanted, if this were merely its way of letting her know it would not accept her after all.

A week later, she set out, telling others no details, saying only that she was following the guidance of one of the seers and was not to be followed.

Although Rowena was a cultured woman, she was practical and austere, and also recently experienced in various purgings of the flesh undertaken in her efforts on behalf of the kingdom. So the snow's cold did not penetrate her sturdy boots, nor did fear of it make her tremble, and she walked quite steadily until the deepening gloom suggested a very late hour indeed.

She had formulated an approach to her fear and dislike of the forest which she relied upon consistently as she progressed: the trees were strong, and filled with wildnesses unspoken, but the people were also strong, and had dwelt on the land for many generations. The animal-people of which she had heard were never seen here; they and the trees and all the animals were being subdued, they would not interfere with her if she did not *show* her fear. By behaving as if she was unconcerned and competent, and by believing in the effectiveness of this behavior, she would be able to progress unmolested.

This was exactly what transpired, well into the dead of night.

But of course there was no accounting in her calculations for the psychological power of the forest at such a deep point, far from hearth or any other human heart. When she sat to rest at last, contemplating making a nest for herself until dawn, the very air itself seemed to be pulsing intimately. There were a few little noises near and far, but aside from these a silence prevailed that made her uncomfortable, made her feel strange impulses to shout every once in a while. She still exerted outward control, but her heart and thoughts were racing.

She wondered how many creatures were observing her. When her thoughts drifted, she would find them expanding outward through the trees, sliding between the slender waists and the sturdy ones, the limbs and claws and vines unnumbered and untold, outward, until her mind shuddered at the enormity and she would have to pull it back in. She rose and continued long past the time limit allotted for sleep in her schedule. After an unimaginable interval, she happened to glance up from her path, and noticed something she realized she had been seeing for some time: a pale lace interspersed amongst the topmost branches. With a shock she realized this was daylight. She stopped, craning her neck upward. Was this all the light the day provided in this ghastly place? She slumped wearily where she stood, the shock giving way to panting and tears as she rubbed her cold face.

Suddenly she froze, not breathing at all, at a high keening issuing from a place so near that all the hairs on her body raised themselves. The sound climbed and leveled and moved higher and higher, unbearably, then slowly fell over many beats of her heart, and her ears strained after it in the silence.

Then, arising out of the night with a shocking familiarity, a voice said, "Do not fear." It was gravelly and strange, but also yearning and gentle. She instantly felt relief but then, suddenly, complete uncertainty. How could she have thought she knew that voice, for it was indeed as strange to her as it should be in the middle of the forest.

"Who are you?" she asked, grateful for her disciplined body, her clear voice and self-possession, for she was very afraid.

Silence.

"I am not afraid, only weary," she bluffed. "Do you intend to challenge me? Speak now if you do."

Silence. She rose and began walking again, her mind spinning. Should she leave the trail? Out in the open, she was so vulnerable to this stranger, and she thought she could feel his gaze on her quite tangibly.

After a while, she did leave the trail, veering off into one of the periodic smaller branchings she could glimpse through the darkness on either side. She sank down again in an overpowering desire to be unseen, to be still, and to give her observer the opportunity to confront her if he so chose. She pulled her bulky wrap from around her pack, draped it over herself, and rested against a tree.

She dozed, passing in and out of sleep. At length she rose and stepped to her left, where she found a little grate with a red little fire going, inside a little room carved in a tree, but the fire gave no heat when she reached down to it. She awoke, dozed again, and looked over at the young woman sleeping beside her, a girl with exquisite yellow curls and smiling sky-blue eyes Rowena could see although the girl kept them closed. Rowena wanted very much to protect this tart yellow butterfly, and yet she was consumed with anxiety that her strength and wits would be inadequate. The girl then awoke, stretched and smiled at Rowena, and was up and gone, stepping through a tangle of bushes and rocks. Somehow Rowena followed, stepping over and through to a clearing. There stood the girl, but she was now a man, large and gray and old, but kind. His eyes were blue, were in fact the same eyes as the girl's, so that looking into them, Rowena could still see her. He gazed at her sympathetically but didn't seem upset. "There, there, my dear, a nice cup of tea ought to get us out of this," he said, and she was flooded with feelings of warmth and shelter, and yearned toward this big kindly man with all her heart. He gestured to the little grate at his feet and it flared briefly. Looking back to him, to her horror she watched his gray hair thicken and luxuriate outward, spreading to erupt from his skin as well to form a thick gray pelt. His ears and mouth and nose grew and changed, and she knew he was an animal-man, a man-wolf. It raised its paw to her placatingly, "Do not fear," it sighed mournfully, but it could not hide its soft snarl of frustration, or its sharp white teeth, and its mouth widened to a scarlet O. She froze in ice-hot terror, her mind retreating, for Rowena was not a screamer. "If I do not show fear..." she repeated to herself by reflex, at the same time saying, "Down its gullet I shall go, the circle of red the way will show..." She was almost relieved, for she felt sure the creature would be mercifully quick. When it did not move, she finally turned to run, but saw to her horror that she was slogging through thick mud and there were leeches everywhere.

She awoke with a loud, mewling yelp and her first feeling was one of embarrassment, followed by leechless relief, before the darkness bore in again.

She sat still, the images from her dream running through her mind. The little rest had done her good, her mind was clear and she was not so frightened. Heed your dreams, the seer had said, so she took care to fasten the details to memory before they melted away.

Rowena continued along the new trail. She was now in a part of the forest that might see one traveler every hundred years. The trail climbed, and the air lightened slightly, but there was also snow. By the time she dropped to her knees beside a tree to settle for the night the cold was bitter and the snow plentiful.

When she rose again, the night was very black and she had difficulty moving. She was weary, and could barely swallow the bit of dry meat and the drops of melted snow that formed her breakfast. She wondered if the creature, for she believed it to be a man-wolf as in her dream, was still following her: she had heard nothing of it, but imagined dully that she could still sense its presence. Slowly, she reflected that since her encounter with it and the subsequent dream, she'd given little thought to the possibility of any other attacker.

She wondered about the one she was to meet, and the circle of red. She wondered if she was becoming too lethargic, if she ought to build a fire despite the risk, but she made no move to do so, and trudged on.

Many hours later, she leaned against a tree, suddenly come back to herself, realizing she was very cold and weak indeed; her heart began working harder, driving home the fact that she needed warmth and rest, and soon. She dropped her pack and began making the motions necessary to strike camp, but snow was drifting down now and she could barely move. She thought of the creature out there somewhere, and leaned against the tree again, faint.

Opening her eyes, she glimpsed a tiny light ahead. Pulling on her wrap but dropping her pack, she moved slowly, blinking at the snow, toward it.

She came to a mighty fire, blindingly bright, set out in the midst of a camp. Six little woodland animals, skinned, gutted and still steaming, lay skewerd beside a log, ready to cook. The area was swept clean of snow. But what made Rowena's mouth drop open in a misty gasp, was the wreath of roses strewn in a ring around the fire, dozens of them, beautifully arranged. Deepest maroon, just as in her gardens at home, her prize bed.

She knew she might be dreaming, and she knew that if this was an enchantment there were procedures she ought to follow, but she was so weary, she merely walked slowly into the circle, over to the fire, and sank down to warm herself.

The fire gave her strength, and she eventually cooked and ate the animals, carefully setting one aside for any visitor, friend or foe, then returned to the path to retrieve her pack. Her eyes and ears continually scanned the blackness surrounding the ring, but there was nothing, not even snow. Lulled by her comfort, she began entertaining fantasies of a protective shell of blackness surrounding her, imagining that the forest bent its limbs over her in caress and concern. She dozed, sitting back against a tree, staring into the flame.

When the figure stepped into her vision across the fire, at first she did not react. Certain she was dreaming, she studied it in fascination: a wolf, and yet man, and the eye was astounded at the simplicity of the blend. Shortened muzzle; paws extending into graceful, slender black-padded fingers; feral, intelligent eyes; deep blue skin beneath the fur. She had never seen an animal-man close up, had never wanted to, and was glad for the dream, which was giving her the opportunity to accustom herself to the way one looked in case the one who had spoken to her earlier turned up again. If it had been following her, the fire had temporarily frightened it away, she reasoned. That was good, for she wanted nothing to interfere with her meeting with the man who walked at night, who had obviously prepared the ring, who would now come to her.

The creature, very vivid to her now (so vivid for a dream!), stepped slowly round to her, crouching low, until it was quite close. Its eyes were blue and yellow, and she looked deeply into them, and found it as easy as falling into a pond on a summer's day...

Slowly the realization came that this was no dream, and although outwardly still, panic began to rouse her. She smelled the wild odor of wolf and clover and stream, but the creature's breath was clean and hot. She held its eyes, although that had become very frightening. Slowly, the creature raised its paw to touch a long black finger to her face and she shrank back, unable to withstand its touch.

She saw the sadness cross its face. "Do not fear," it implored again, and the sight of the mouth moving and the sound of the words emerging was so eerie and horrible that she grew dizzy.

"I will not harm you," it insisted.

"What is it that you want?" she finally whispered.

It did not answer, but, after a moment, yearning suffusing its features, it raised a hand again to her face.

Dreadful comprehension impelled her to her feet. She stepped away a little and turned to face the creature, which continued to kneel. "You must leave," she said firmly, in a blend of the way she would speak to her dog and her servant. "Someone is coming, do you understand? He will kill you if you harm me." She stood her ground, and they stared into each others' eyes.

Slowly, the creature rose until it was at its full height, well over hers. Its face was inscrutable. It pointed at its breast. "I am the one."

Shocked, she took a step back. "You are not."

This had an impact: the creature wavered a little.

"The one who laid this camp," she gestured, encouraged, "he is the one returning, he is the one for whom I wait."

Suddenly, the creature seemed to understand something, and its tongue lolled out to pant, but she also had the distinct impression it was amused. Again it gestured to its breast, then at the camp. It touched its nose. "You cannot smell," it said knowingly.

Smell? she wondered. Smell what? "Of course I can smell," she said impatiently. But even as she spoke she understood: to this creature's senses, a scent-signature was obvious, inarguable. And that meant—but she would not let herself follow the thought to its full meaning and began gathering and cleaning her things to distract herself.

The creature sat back on its haunches, watching her. She glanced at it surreptitiously and thought it looked contented for the time being, although its eyes so constant upon her were very unnerving. She came to the animal she had set aside, and, on impulse, offered it to the creature. It accepted the food solemnly, and snapped it down. She sat down a few feet away, cleaning her teeth, and they regarded each other.

"Do you have a name?" she asked.

It narrowed its eyes in that sly, amused way. "Beloved," it said after a moment.

She curled her lip. An irritating coincidence that this creature would mouth that particular word, a word with special meaning to her, a word that had come from dreams she didn't even remember.

"I can't call you that. Don't you have another, real name?"

"Not exactly," it said. Apologetic, mischievous, it rose and began to pace, flicking its eyes here and there but always returning to her. She looked at it curiously but it immediately swelled with pride so she looked away. She was beginning to grasp its empathetic abilities and found them disturbing.

The creature darted out of the ring and back in with more wood for the fire.

It moved in nearer to her, inhaling her scent and looking closely at her from all around.

She sat quietly, but the creature's sudden pungent, pressing presence so close to her was stirring dread within her belly, and at last she faced the truth: surely the roses comprised the circle of red, and surely the creature could be construed as the one who walked at night. Since it seemed to have one and only one intent with her, was mating with this creature her special doom?

She could not see past this, and made no move to quiet the increasingly agitated creature. Regardless of whether she was meant to commit this act, it seemed it would occur anyway.

She covered her face. What had she done to deserve such humiliation?

She felt it approach then, its motions suddenly quiet. She felt it touch her hair, gently stroking it. Her tears poured out gratefully.

"Ah...you have not been taken," it breathed into her ear, explaining that it suddenly understood.

She dropped her hands in exasperation, pride sparking a temporary flash of self-possession. What was the matter with the thing, "Not been taken?"

"I am the queen of this land. I have been wed to its king for many years," she said, shuddering as she inhaled the creature's scent.

It moved to face her, looking into her eyes. "You have not been taken," it said again with amusement, amazement, and utter certainty. She fell into its eyes again, summer yellow and blue and deep cool wells of black. She saw the old man there, and felt the creature as a man for the first time, and not merely as an animal; she felt his subtlety and power, and was revulsed, but also thrilled.

The creature waited, his nostrils moving as they tasted a whiff of her desire. There was a moment of intimacy the like of which she had never before experienced as she simply felt her own desire and that of the creature; she felt *his* comfortable, happy acceptance of it, at least, if not her own.

He slowly reached up to her throat, and she stopped his hand before he touched her, to examine his darkness and fur, and tapering, limber fingers, with the claws bitten off, for her, she knew. She looked back into his eyes, felt their wonder and fascination with her, glimpsed the alien soul inside.

Slowly and eagerly, he trailed his fingers down her throat and breast, down to her belly, where he pressed and stroked her, kneaded her. Suddenly he groaned and pressed into her, cradling her groin and pinning her with an exultant growl, but she twisted away and ran back down the trail.

She ran a long way, lost and seeking the main trail amidst a patchwork of narrower ones. She fell a few times and each time the creature approached her in a pained submissive manner, and each time she pushed him away. The last time, she could not move, and she was unconscious, her system overcome by cold, exhaustion and fear, before he could collect her.

She awoke nude, surrounded by warm fur and blackness. The creature's vulpine tongue caressed her body, and she knew he did this just as her bitch licked her pups, impersonally, eyes ruminatively shut. She pretended to remain sleeping, but the creature immediately stopped, and she could feel him watching her in the darkness.

Eventually, tentatively, he began licking her again. She shut her eyes, and resigned herself, knowing she had given consent.

Head to toe the creature went then, inch by painful inch. Rowena's thoughts wandered near and far, the creature's tongue the anchor to them all. Quickly the images flitted at first; brief, horrible pictures of what he might do, bestial and painful, led to memories of incidents with her husband, unpleasant incidents that had provoked similar feelings in her. The way that the prize dog had mated with her bitch, the glimpsed and overheard pokings and winks and rubbings between people she had witnessed her whole life and always despised: humankind was meant to rise above all that was bestial. When she remembered the way her husband submitted to her requirements, she momentarily tensed, because she had a feeling this creature would take no conditions. He paused again, and she felt his breath on her arm. Her skin was glowing, and it missed his tongue. He resumed this time more confidently.

"How did you come to—find me?" she asked. She could hear that the den was very small.

He slowed and paused, and moved his mouth close to her ear. "I have known you long, long hours from before," he whispered, and when she heard the emotion suffusing his voice, a breach was made in her stony defense, for his love was as naked as her body.

"What do you mean?" she asked, letting the warmth creep a little into her voice.

They lay almost side by side and she felt the thrill of excitement run through him. He carefully contained it though, and contented himself with nuzzling her ear. "The hours you spend with...beloved," he whispered.

She froze, mortified. Flames seemed to surround her, blending with the heat from the fur and the tongue of this creature. Her dreams, curled in the covers of her huge queenly bed, the world locked away..."How—how could you—how could you know?" The tongue passed over a breast, paused, and she felt the creature's nose linger, breathing, a hairsbreadth from her nipple, then the tongue passed over it again, and repeated again slowly, reflectively.

"I do not know," it breathed onto her breast. "I find you when you go to one of your places. The sand and sea among the waves, or the stony villa, or the enchanted garden with the heated pool..." his voice broke and he vented a peculiar high, moaning sigh. She almost laughed, but restrained herself, marveling.

"Are you only a dream, then?" she asked, wishing her nipple were not so responsive to his coaxing, feeling its beeline connection to her groin and womb.

"I come for your desire," he snarled after a long, long while. His voice was broken but her mind was having trouble following it anyway, and did not bother to put it back together. The creature's long tongue began curling up and around between her thighs, and coaxed her finally to murmur his name into the darkness.

Rowena spent some period of days with the creature, and thought nothing of her kingdom. After joining with her, the creature seemed to know her every thought and feeling even better. This, with his quickness and playfulness, made him like a second self of hers, different and with independent will, but like a light within her mind, always there. The intensity of his pleasure when she first placed her hand upon him thrilled her; she eagerly explored his weaknesses and special spots of delight, and manipulated them with growing skill and relish. She watched her old, sad self retreating from her, and sympathetically waved goodbye.

During this time she wasn't surprised to find the spring arrive. She smiled when she thought of how she would reward the grouchy old woman, and what unforeseen pleasures the hag and her niece would enjoy in their old age.

The last night, the creature placed his hand on her womb. "It is done," he whispered reverently, but with proud amazement. There was a peculiar dreamy sadness then between them; she realized she would return home in the morning, but felt quite calm.

This time between them would never return, she thought as they lingered together just inside the forest the next morning. But surely fate would somehow permit them to be together again in some way, and, she had her dreams...

She was greeted with appropriate salutations, for there was no doubt in anyone's mind that her successful quest was responsible for the thaw. Many observed out of the corner of their eyes the redness of her lips, the moisture in her eyes, and many other small differences, and, of course, wondered, but she cheerfully refused to disclose her experiences.

In the midst of preparations for a celebratory feast that evening, she inquired after her husband, whom she had not yet seen.

"He is well," her maid Ruth told her as they arranged candles and garlands at the head table. "He keeps to himself more than ever, milady," glancing at her appraisingly.

"Be sure he is there tonight," she said evenly, but inwardly suffering twinges of guilt, not only for her recent passion with another, but for all her years of coldness to him.

"He shall be, as long as the feasting starts before dusk," said Ruth, interested by her mistress' tone and drawing out the conversation to learn as much as she told.

"Oh, does he retire so early?"

"Yes, but what's worse, he's taken to wandering in his sleep each night since you've been gone."

Rowena paused. "Wandering?"

"Yes m'lady. Walking at night in his sleep."

"Walking at night in his sleep," she repeated. Neither woman worked now, Ruth looking at Rowena, Rowena looking away. "Wandering. Where does he go?"

"No one knows, m'lady. He'll allow no guard posted, insists upon this although he cares little for anything else by day. Eats and sleeps, mostly. Perhaps he'll stop now that you're home, m'lady," she inserted meaningfully.

Rowena caught her meaning and collected herself. "Perhaps he will. Thank you, Ruth." Her beloved creature's rhythmic disappearances from the den, her arrival home in a mere hour's time astride the creature's back.... Soon Rowena made no pretense at working, and uncharacteristically leaving her staff to finish, she retired to the rose garden to think.

That evening, there were few who didn't notice the change in their queen. Things didn't go absolutely smoothly, but she was so relaxed, so pleasant, that the people enjoyed themselves more than at previous events run with greater precision.

Most striking was her sweet and infectious treatment of her husband the king. After staring at her as she eyed him and pressed against him, he began to respond, straightening and smiling, a wilted, dusky flower rescued by a last summer rain. By the end of the long evening's river of wine, they sat peering into each other's eyes. As everyone else drifted contentedly away, the soul within his eyes began to awaken.

"Beloved," she whispered happily, and nuzzled his palm.

He narrowed his eyes and smiled at her in a look familiar from a different face. She playfully disentangled and sauntered out to the garden.

She lingered there, wandering amongst the new roses. After a while, she became drowsy and dreaming. The air grew misty and rain began to fall. In the shelter of the gazebo, she sank down upon a cushion, soaking up the sensations. She heard a hundred popping sounds, and looked about with amazement at plants all around her sprouting and blooming quickly enough to watch. There was a feeling of enchantment in the air, and then she felt a presence...

She did not turn, afraid to break the spell. She felt him creep up behind her, felt him lightly cup her shoulders. She looked down and saw no black and furry tapering fingers, just the freckled hands of her husband. And yet, how strong and sure they were! She turned and looked up into his face, and smiled at her friend from the forest, her friend from her dreams; they smiled at their own not knowing, at all the lost memories, forbidden dreams and shunned intentions.

They smiled mostly, however, at the time yet before them.

Eleven

It is spring. A cave sits in a high place overlooking a lush valley, and the view from its mouth takes in a breathless sun-painted vision of green, a fresh delicacy not seen in any other world or time. Violets favor the ledge beneath this cave; they have made it their permanent vacation resort, and can be seen basking luxuriously day after day.

A fragment of sunlight appears bobbing up the path within sight of the cave. It floats atop a round, glowing moon-shape, and now can also be seen the sweet blue eyes and the rosebud mouth adorning its surface, classic and fresh, like the violets.

This lovely young mortal comes up to the cave-ledge and pauses. She looks out over the valley, then turns to the cave shyly, as if it is a sentient being she has come to see. Her face is a tangle of emotions for one of such a simple and innocent people, people at the first bursting out of a new age, not yet given to melancholy reflection. Hope, apprehension, curiosity, frustration, long patience and, what must be the hub of this wheel, love. Not quite unrequited, not quite fulfilled.

A hoped-for dalliance? She touches the mouth of the cave and looks and steps in, her eyes moving about it in half-darting, half-searching movements. There is a faint glow from the heated pool within, and as the shadows drape around her, she looks darker, older, and more serious. It seems she is already disappointed, but that the disappointment was expected and she is carrying on.

She goes about lighting the fragrant oil pots scattered around the cave, and with each flame leaps into sight a different amazement. Many, many groups of flowers of all varieties, arranged in many ways: figures, designs, carousels and little bridges over little flower rivers. All the nuts and cones and glitter-rocks and shiny insect wings native to her land find their places and hold hands in design, danced and interwoven at the beckoning of this mortal girl's dreamy, steady fingers. Wreaths and hanging gardens, mosaics, collages and paintings cover the warm, dry walls. In one place six small woodland animals, of a kind considered a delicacy by her people, lie strung on an altar. It seems she cannot bear looking at them, this untouched offering.

Slowly she moves around, replacing the flowers that have wilted with new ones, touching and moving designs dreamily, singing softly to herself. All that she feels suffuses the cave with her voice.

When there is nothing left to do, when the cave is settled to her satisfaction with its romping, tumbling beauty, she stands by the pool looking around absently, then sinks to sit beside it with a sigh.

Who is so heartless as to neglect such devotion?

She runs her finger over the water and looks into its depths. "You are not here," she breathes, the words obviously fragments of her heart, broken and cast off now as useless. It all seems too deep even for tears, and she droops, sinking into herself.

This cave is very high, but no so deep. Spread across the back wall the girl has created a being of deep blue, of her own design. It is not a literal drawing, it is rather a special space invested with all her most heart-felt emotions and objects. There are wolflike ears and a wolflike grace of line; a stag's antlers and the rays of the sun; glittering rain; strands of the girl's shining hair; the most precious gems and seashells from far away. The pair of eyes are the most clearly drawn aspect, not mortal nor animal, but the penetrating and truly drawn eyes of a god. Beneath this is her altar.

The girl chose this spot the way a bitch chooses where to pup or to pee: in a fever of yearning, she had paced and circled the cave, narrowing down to two or three spots, and then finally rubbing her body against this one, keening and moaning. Face, breasts, belly and groin were pressed and rubbed on the wall, and then buttocks and thighs in as coquettish a mating posture as she knew. Next a full coat of her menstrual blood was smeared over the spot to let the god know she was able. Then came the design, which she worked on only in times of emotional heights, with reverence and with a mixture of tribal and original ritual. When she stood there, she felt she was bathing in his vision, a wonderful warm splashing all over her body. When she wept for him, she pressed her breasts and aching heart against the wall, pressed her face to his eyes, to share her tears.

The girl had chosen well. Behind the eyes of her god, through the wall, exists a lovely, dim, musical place, with a large round comfortable chair for observation. It has existed there since many long years before the birth of the girl's grandparents. The floor is warm sand, with exquisite mobiles and shivering little fountains scattered about, of a striking transparency, fragility, and sophistication when juxtaposed with the florid arrangements just on the other side. Each construct has its subtle musical counterpart entwined.

From this inner compartment the outer cave can be seen through the wall with complete clarity. As the mortal stands before her altar and looks into the eyes she has created on the wall, she looks unwittingly with a lovely geometrical precision directly into the eyes of whomever sits in the chair.

A being has been accustomed to sit in this chair for many years prior to the girl's birth. The race to which this being belongs has a longer lifespan than humans, a different conception of time actually, and he is rather old even within that framework. His form and movement are of such finer substance, readily apparent, than the sturdy, fleshy humans that it is little wonder he and his kind are regarded as gods.

Mind and brain are fused to a great extent in these beings, lending their ways and their physical creations a dreamlike, intangible quality to the perception of humans, what with other realities so cunningly and sophisticatedly integrated into this one.

Correlating with this development, this race chose long ago to tame and effectively hobble the urge to excel in physical strength, as humans have not. Coinciding therefore with the flowering of this civilization, couched comfortably within its safe and aesthetic systems of underground cities, tunnels, and outposts, came a decline, a falling-away, of active physical power. Among most there is aversion to it, rooted in fear of their vulnerability. Now, having evolved past the need for the schoolroom of physical reality, the race is in the gradual process of leaving the Earth entirely.

Only the hardier souls choose to work in the outposts, observing and telepathically teaching and guiding the fledgling human species.

The being in this outpost has formed telepathic relationships with many sensitive individual humans through the years, and everyone on both sides of the wall is pleased with the blossoming of the human culture within the reach of his tuteledge.

As the girl sits dispiritedly by the pool, this being sits watching her in an equally pensive mood, his long blue fingers steepled beneath his nose, his elbows propped on the arms of his chair.

Another being now comes silently up from within the tunnel leading away from the cave, and gently puts his hands on the younger god's shoulders.

"Josef," he says softly, and Josef reaches back and clasps the older one's hand as it rests on his shoulder. They stay thus for a while, looking out into the outer cave. Josef's sadness would be tangible even to a human, regardless of the absence of tears in the alien red eyes.

Finally he rises with a great sigh, and turns to embrace his friend. Leaning, they remain thus holding each other close. "Thank you for coming," Josef says with great emotion. The elder places his hand on Josef's head in a universal gesture of tenderness and benediction. They pull back and search each other's eyes. The elder's expression is compassionate, but also very slightly amused.

With a couple of languid motions they have reformed the chair to accommodate both of them, and they resume the vigil.

The girl lifts her face to them, cocking an ear, then droops again.

"I understand more now," says the elder after he has watched her. She begins singing again, and the soft, plaintive tones float into the room. "Your decision will be important to her...and to you," he says, looking slyly at Josef.

Josef returns the look wryly, then his eyes drift back to the mortal, as always.

"I don't know," he says after another long interval, "why I can't understand this. I knew this girl was familiar, from dreams of her, before she was even born. Within the Greater Realm, therefore, we are already companions. I...know that I love her. And yet, my dread and unwillingness to enter her world are as potent as ever. Perhaps more so, now that I am near the end of my stay. How can these two truths be?"

The elder settles back philosophically, and ponders, or pretends to do so. "Perhaps...one is a truth, and one is only a fear."

Josef acknowledges this with silence, although he is not terribly pleased. "All my life, I have had a primary desire to avoid mingling within their culture. I did not seek her out. By the Earth, I was eager for the end of my stay, Karel! To rejoin you and the others.... It is not only fear, therefore."

"I know this, my dear friend." He is a little apologetic.

"Now, if I join with her, a part of me will be locked within their reality for centuries," Josef continues moodily. "You have seen the broad outlines of what that reality would entail. Violent, restrictive..."

"Innovative and adventuresome..."

"It is not to my taste." Josef's eyes, however, follow the girl as she rises and begins to pace, then to twirl and sway a little. His breathing alters, and the elder smiles to himself.

"With such a companion along your way..." the elder murmurs, captivated as well.

"She is gentle and graceful now, for she senses my need for it. Among her own kind she plays the same harsh games, fights and kills, tumbles all about in reckless abandon just like the rest of her people."

"Of which are you more afraid, her or the race?" the elder asks curiously.

Josef thinks a while, interested in the question. He softens as he continues watching her. "I do not fear her," he says at last.

The elder waits a moment before saying gently, "This will be good for you, Josef."

Josef sighs.

"As far as you have come, you are still limited by your unwillingness to venture alone into alien realities. Your abilities will expand immeasurably when your faith in the benevolence of the raw universe is strengthened."

"You still feel so," Josef sighs again.

"Feel for the resonance of this truth within your love for this girl, and you will see no further dichotomy."

Josef is still. His emotion swells and fills the room again. The girl pauses, and, looking toward her god, she walks up and presses herself to his image on the wall.

"She is remarkable," breathes the elder.

"She has always been so," says Josef. It is difficult for him to speak, but the pressure of his feeling begs release. "She stands out among the others in her tribe, and although they respect her, she feels great loneliness at times."

The elder wisely says nothing, regarding his friend again quietly.

"From the beginning," Josef says once more with wry amusement, "she would not be content with the traditional relationship with me. She thought she hid her feelings well for quite some time, and went about our work with zeal. Perhaps if I had withdrawn then...but...I was drawn to her as well, as you know.... Our dreams together—I have never experienced such...such...."

The elder lays a hand upon his arm gently in understanding.

"I had to be nimble to keep a step ahead of her, to retain the tutelary relationship, when from the beginning I was tempted to permit myself to slow my pace and dally with her, to close away the world and..." his voice breaks as he shuts his eyes, swept by emotion.

The woman moans and rocks, and her voice escalates into a loud cry of pain. She turns roughly and paces. She grabs a sharp little shell and drops to her knees before her altar. Crying angrily, looking up into her god's painted eyes, she flashes forth her wrist in an obvious gesture.

"Speak to her, Josef," the elder murmurs.

"Tera," whispers Josef.

Her face clears triumphantly for a moment, and she lowers her wrist, still looking up, a little defiant.

"Tera, what are you doing," he scolds affectionately.

She lowers her face, biting her lip, briefly subdued, then looks up. "You have not come," she blurts out.

Josef rises and steps to a point closer to the invisible wall, where his eyes meet Tera's exactly, with hers at their upward facing angle. He says nothing, but her face clears again, and a peace spreads over her features. She shuts her eyes and leans back on her heels, her hands knotted between her thighs. Her body is lithe and voluptuous. They remain so for a time.

He places his hand on the wall. After a moment, she opens her eyes, and slowly rises, and places her hand at the same spot on her side of the wall, so that their palms would touch without the rock between them. The spot coincides with the place where the god's heart would be, were it depicted. She leans pensively, stroking the spot with a very small motion, and the elder lets out a long quiet breath of amazement as Josef leans closer as well. They stand thus for another long stretch of time.

"It is time, Josef," says the elder.

She speaks almost at the same moment, "Should I not come back?" she asks quietly, but her tears are copious.

"I needed to be sure you understand, little one," Josef whispers.

"I understand," she says, hope brightening her face a little. "I know my life will change, my thoughts, my heart—that I will feel a loneliness for you...but, that our son will give me comfort and happiness, and remind me of you. Is that right?"

He doesn't answer, but places his palm where her face is. She seems to feel the warmth there, for she places her cheek against it. "Why are you so sad?" she asks.

He strokes the place where her cheek presses, with the same small motion she had used. For a moment he is too overcome to answer. "Your people regard us as gods. It is true, we are very different from you, older, perhaps wiser in ways. Yet—we are not omnipotent. We are a gentle people, we work with our hearts and our minds more than with our hands. Your people are young, and very strong. Although you will accomplish much through the ages of your dominion, much that we did not, there is also much for you to learn. With my seed passing into your race, a part of myself enters it, and must remain within it for the requisite number of incarnations until it learns what your race needs to learn, and what I need to learn as a physical human personality. I...am fearful of the bruises and struggles that must be undergone by this strand of myself. I am very, very old, little one, and I am weary of physical existence to a certain extent. I had not anticipated extending it."

She has been silent, head cocked, listening to his voice within her with full attention. She does not move now, thinking. She lowers her head. "It is my fault, for being so immoderate."

"That is not correct, little one. The fear is my weakness, one I have needed to work on within my native system of reality, a certain tendency to hold myself aloof.... Like you, I have things to learn as well if I am to grow.... Your people's robust, reckless pursuit of physical life is a good test for me to develop a feeling of surety even as a stranger within it. Do you understand?"

She nods, then shrugs, and smiles shyly. "It is hard to believe you have any flaws. It seems to me you know everything, that you are nothing but kindness and...wisdom."

"I am older than you, but in the Greater Realm, we are equals, as all beings everywhere are. You understand this somewhat from your dreams."

She nods again.

"Think of your desire for me," he continues, "and know that mine for you burns fully equally, and that is more important a parity than any amount of skill or strength."

She looks up then, and they stand eye to eye, the painted eyes still hovering between them. She says tenderly, protectively, "I know my people are low and rough, but I shall not harm you. I feel already...changed, from since I knew you. Do you believe me? I will do all as you explained to me. Do you believe me?"

He does not answer, but gazes into her eyes so intensely that she breathes deeply and almost quails. She leans against the wall.

"You are fertile tomorrow night?" he asks.

Suddenly not brazen anymore, she blushes a full red. "Yes," she murmurs with a tiny embarrassed smile, looking down. "If I come here, and lie in darkness and readiness as you said...will it be possible...for you to..."

"That would be possible," he breathes finally.

She is overcome, but very still. "Tomorrow night?" she repeats in wonder, in a small voice.

"Tomorrow night, my love," he says.

She looks at him a moment more, her face transfigured, and she is just a mortal girl on the eve of her awakening, excited, wondering, all these emotions blended. She beams at him, and the air itself seems likely to burst into flame with their fire before she backs away and then, after a last look at him, dashes out with a squeal.

"You are certain of this?" the elder asks Josef.

"Almost certain," he replies. It is dusk of the fated evening, and they lounge on a low curved couch on the floor, sipping juice. Josef is agitated, although he contains this as always. He has become aware of a disturbing new intention on the part of Tera.

The elder turns away.

"You find this amusing," Josef says, perturbed and surprised.

"I am sorry, my dear one. It's just that if I were to have previously imagined the female who would so entrance you, I would have expected just such a one as this, full of challenge and defiance. Like you. It reminds me of when *I* was *your* teacher," says the elder, more amused with every moment.

"She has heard the stories of what happens when a mortal sees the face of a Lumarian lover. She knows the risk to herself. For that matter, she knows my reluctance to enter her reality in such a manner."

"She would not be the person she is—and you would without doubt not be with her!—was she not possessed of spirit that seeks the core of any experience. I am surprised you did not expect this!"

"Surely I must prevent it. I can take the match from her beforehand. She will not disobey."

The elder pauses. "Think clearly, my friend. When you

step into that cave, you leave behind your authority as teacher, and walk nakedly as lover, as equal, as all true love must. If you confront her with your knowledge, acquired through prescience she does not possess, and control the entire experience therewith, what will be the effect upon the act?"

Josef closes his eyes for several minutes. When he opens them, he rises and walks to the back of the cave, staring into the tunnel. "It is almost not worth doing."

"As I suspected. You are seeing everything only through your lens of fear, and any solution therefrom is bound to be damaging. Step outside it a moment. Forget how distasteful you believe you think their culture to be. Perceive her true intentions, her true desires and feelings. Are they mischievous defiance only?"

Josef closes his eyes again for another bracket of minutes. By the time he opens them, his breathing has quieted. He turns to his friend, a little sheepish, but grateful.

"I ask you this question only," Karel says, walking up to him. "Is she truly aware of the meaning of her action? To the extent that she has a chance of surviving it intact?"

"She is. She is very afraid, and also feels quite guilty. But there is a desperation, and...and feelings of challenge and certainty." Josef is amused now, incredulous yet again at what he has on his hands.

"Who are you to take this responsibility of choice from her hands? Who are you to deny her self-expression within the most important experience of her life? Do I need to tell you the consequences as well as presuming to know better than she what is best for her in this area? Most interesting of all, has it occurred to you that, knowing you as she does, she just may be acting in a clearer, more beneficial way for you as well, following her own instinct and desire unclouded by your weighty fears?"

Josef has absorbed all this with difficulty, and when Karel is finished he moves around to sit again in the big chair. He sighs heavily. "I am not able to think with complete clarity, Karel. But I believe you are right."

The elder moves to him and places his hands on his shoulders again. Josef closes his eyes and leans back. Karel strokes his face. "Try not to focus so on the distasteful aspects of this system. Remember, when you join corporally with her now and in the future, it shall transcend even what you have experienced with her in the dream world, in its way, and this is true of this reality as a whole. Until you find the inner voice, yes, there is much conflict. But you will find it, in each lifetime, and subsequently all trouble will be experienced as adventure, albeit still reluctantly, I imagine."

Silence again, as the elder calms his beloved.

"How shall I prevent her from disengaging when she sees my visage?"

The elder drops his hands and walks to the invisible wall. "I have been considering that. Perhaps I could be present."

"Surely that would only compound her fear."

"I am not her lover: I need not appear in my true form, as you must. I could appear as someone human and reassuring to her, but also someone she respects enough to obey during those first crucial minutes."

Josef considers this. "I see. Whom would you be?"

"We could dream together for a period of time, and I could seek out a visage from a future life of hers, one you will wear. Or..."

Josef looks at his friend curiously. "Or what?"

"I have been considering...perhaps I shall enter this reality with you."

"What?" Josef is shocked.

"I have passed through it once already, it shall not be terribly uncomfortable. I shall incarnate with the two of you each time, to observe firsthand, so to speak. It shall be an adventure!"

"You are a strange fellow, Karel. Strange and crafty. Fortunately for me."

"I feel a glimmer of one such personality," the elder says, closing his eyes, pleased. "A female, I believe, close to both of you in a very potent time. Come, let us dream a while together, and I will fix on a visage."

"Tera."

She opens her eyes in the darkness. The thrill she is feeling as she senses the dark shape approaching her is understandable, but she has spent an hour in the soothing exercises taught her by Josef, and her fear is minimal. "I am here."

The presence is a cool breeze and a warm, pulsing glow; it moves with eye blinking swiftness but slow as a stalking panther. Darkness moves with it, dampening even the faint whiteness from starlight outside and the pale green fizz from the pool. Finally she knows he is at her side.

"You look as if you are on your funeral bier," he says with a smile in his voice. "Sit up and speak with me a while."

She lets out a small breath of laughter, tension evaporating. "All right," and slowly sits up. She feels him rest his weight beside her, not very close.

"You are very beautiful," he breathes.

She looks down reflexively, and pulls her arms in close, tightening her legs, nervously smiling.

"Are you cold?" he asks.

"No."

"Then open yourself and let me look at you."

She obeys, and feels her tension drain away as it is dispossessed by her rekindling desire.

"Better," he says, smiling again.

"You can see me?" A hint of the coquette.

"Very clearly. Can you tell what I am seeing now?"

She closes her eyes to sense his gaze, although it is hardly necessary in the dark. "My throat?"

"Very good. And now?"

"My...arms? my wrists? They're warm..." and she giggles.

"Right again. And what of now?"

It is a moment before she answers now, and when she does her voice trembles. "My eyes?"

"Yes."

More moments pass. "I see and feel the things you said I would..."

"Do you. Tell me what you see and feel."

"It is strange—it is very bright, although I know it is dark..."

"Do not concern yourself with reconciling what seems to be contradiction, do you understand? Simply relax and allow all to flow. There is nothing to harm you."

"Fields! The grass is so green I almost cannot bear it...but I can."

"Of course you can. Your mind is like your body, very strong, but very flexible. If anything becomes uncomfortable, all you need do is close your eyes and pull in, withdraw to yourself and find that center point, and any pressure will be relieved. Do so now." A few moments pass. "Very good. You feel the difference."

"Yes. It's as if you're not here."

"Yes."

"May I come back out now?"

"Of course." Soon she is back basking in the warm glow.

"Your voice is very beautiful."

"Thank you."

"Are you..."

"What?"

"Are you...in human form?"

"For tonight."

"How..."

"I have a form of my own, which you would find difficult to perceive. Tonight, through a certain...focus, I adopt or...overlay more human characteristics onto or into my form. The result is humanlike, and although the experience will seem strange to you, I will be human to your perception."

"Except...if I were to see you."

He pauses slightly. "It's debatable what you would see."

There is a long pause now, as they listen to each other breathe.

"May I...touch you?" she asks, her voice rough.

"Of course."

She leans forward and slowly, slowly reaches over to touch his cheek. She giggles slightly in a tiny gasp. "It's wrinkled and dry but...warm." She traces her fingers over his face very tentatively. "You are very old, aren't you?"

"Yes, my child."

"But in my dreams..."

"Remember: experience, don't reconcile. Both are truths." She gasps and freezes when she feels his fingers on her cheek. "Just as it is true that we fear and desire at once, momentarily."

"You are afraid?"

"Only a little."

"Of what?"

"This is a delicate experience. I wish no harm to come to either of us."

"Don't worry. It'll be all right."

Both of their voices have become weak and dreamy. They stroke each other's faces, then Tera leans over and lightly kisses his cheek, and twines her arms about his neck, and presses herself to him. He gasps at the flood of sensation, then suddenly returns the embrace, feeling a thrill at his own strength. They hold each other, their communication surpassing the limits of articulation, blurring the boundaries between realities.

"Tera, your light has made me see the darkness of my life before you came," he breathes, choking with wonder on an exquisite tightness in his throat.

With that they move apart enough to come face to face, inhaling each other's aromas, tasting the warm mist of each other's breath. The rest is perhaps much the most ancient formula, as fresh and astounding to these two as to any two lovers in any history. With all their movement, they steady on a fine beam between their minds, and wander through various places with near-perfect coalescence. Somehow, as she teaches him the language of the human form, he at once teaches her the language of love's expression.

She almost loses herself, but Tera was Josef's student, and has learned well. She has saved a pocket of her mind sealed against her flooded sense, and even as she sits astride his lap, and they rock with a shivering passion, she reaches to her side, among the unthorned roses comprising her bed, grasps a match, and strikes it on the flinty floor.

In its flare, she freezes as she beholds the face of her lover. "Tera..." he murmurs in agony, and takes her chin to try to hold it firm. Karel appears kneeling at their side, in the aproned form of a matron of some medieval time, and touches their backs in a cradling gesture.

"Look straight into his eyes, little lass, he is the one you've always loved," she says, and her voice is every cherished mother's who ever lived, and not to be doubted.

Saliva drips from a corner of Tera's mouth and her breath comes in animal mewlings, primordial in their horror. Her body is a cold and rigid alabaster. Slowly her eyes move to regard Karel's smiling old moon face, and the ice chips coating them begin to melt.

"That's better," says Karel, beaming at their success. "Now, my dear creature, go to the place where we are all together and all is well, where everything is as it should be, and nothing out of place."

Tera's face relaxes, and ten years of her life melt away in the flickering light from the lamp Karel has lit.

"What is your name, child?"

"C-cathy," she replies in the tongue of that time.

"Cathy, my dear, of course. And you know who I am."

"Lizzie," and she smiles in wonder and relief to have found this contented place, home again at last from a nightmare.

"Aye, my daughter. Now, when you look at your lover, see the one you truly know, for whom you've waited how long?"

"Eighteen months, come midsummer. I thought I'd never last the course!" She wonders at her reluctance to turn her eyes on her love, and yet it is there, a cold hand threatening her heart.

"Look into his eyes now, child, and have no fear."

Slowly she turns her eyes, and fastens them on those of John of Blue, yet even as she sees their green and the glinting red of hair and beard, these things quiver and flicker in and out of sight.

"I know you, I know you," she murmurs with wonder at the kaleidoscope of faces.

"Aye, my dearest love," he replies all tenderly.

" Your skin is truly blue, I see," she says dreamily, perceiving normal flesh and midnight's deepest hue at once beneath her trembling fingers.

"Aye, and does it frighten you?"

"It is strange, 'tis true...the color of the deepest night sky—and yet the sky has never harmed me..."

" 'Tis a sight for these old eyes, to see such a slip of a wench wax so grandly philosophical..."

"Aye, I met a peddler's son once, and wicked as the devil was he, and taught me such devious turnings and twistings of the tongue as would make the Pope himself cross his eyes and tie his ears behind!"

Amid laughter from all three of them, John Blue says, "The seeds grow only on fertile ground, my little saint."

They three prattle on a little bit, then Cathy's face seems to fall into its dream again, out of the clear, warm focus of that time.

" 'Tis strange, I know you well, yet I feel there to be something different, something strange about this place."

"Yes, my love, there is," says Josef, deliberately and gently breaking the dialect and the pace.

Another long while they sit, and slowly,slowly Tera sinks down, down through the protective mists of time, until her inner eye opens once more within the softly glowing cave.

She comes back to herself with a shudder. Josef is strong in his human form, and although it is not comfortable for him to use that strength he holds her hips to him firmly, holds her eyes as well. For many heartbeats more they remain, but each moment is poised for action of any kind.

"Josef," she breathes at last.

"Tera," he says, with narrowed eyes, and there is just enough reproof for her to notice if she chooses.

She does, and looks down in her characteristically mischievous shame. She looks up again, and there is a lightening of her mouth: she wants to smile, but isn't sure if it is appropriate. His expression welcomes it, though, and slowly they take a long sip from the same smile. Halfway through it she jumps.

"My eyes?" asks Josef. "That's right, they glow redder with any passing emotion."

"It's...all right. I can almost...follow it, you know?" She flashes a full smile, and it is his turn to gasp a little at what that conveys. It was one thing to see her on the other side of the wall, and quite another now to smell all her odors, taste her, feel her and feel himself still within her, for coitus is still not yet complete, all while dazzled by full physical sight of her.

She glances to their side. "Who was that?"

"A friend. She was here to help us."

Tera reflects, and grows serious. "You knew that I..."

"Yes, I had a strong idea you would do exactly what you had agreed not to do. I should not have been surprised by it this afternoon."

She feels and accepts the anger that is implicit behind the humor and detachment.

"I'm sorry, Josef." The coquette is gone, leaving only the adult.

"You might have asked me, you know."

She considers this. "Would you have agreed to it?"

His expression, after a moment, bestows another smile upon them both.

Things start to happen then, swellings and nestlings. "Do you regret it?" she asks, now not the coquette nor the adult, but something else again as she leans to him, feeling his hands start to slowly squeeze and knead her hips. In these few minutes she has learned: to stare into his pupils, black as any mortal's, to allay the primal fear of the unknown; that she feels all she ever felt before and more; that her action had deeper meanings and repercussions than she can know right now, more than betrayal, seduction, courage, love or fear, yet containing all of these.

"I might still withdraw, you know," he says. This is a joke, in light of present developments.

"Why did you let me do it?" she asks, still quite serious. Their faces are very close now.

It is long again before he answers, and his voice is broken at last. "Mortal, you shine upon the Earth brighter than the brightest star in any world I have seen..."

"Tell me once more of what lies ahead," she says. "Each time I understand more."

It is the night of the third day, and after cavorting on the hillside and eating, and bathing in the pool, they lie once more upon her bed of roses, freshly laid. Slowly he strokes her belly, resting on an elbow. Like a newborn, his skin has smoothed.

"The eyes are portal to the soul. Had we mated in darkness, my seed only would have passed into your reality."

"Like the giant white wolf—some of his pups are white as well. But the White Wolf himself died long ago, and we see him now only in dreams."

"Yes. Now, with the striking of your match, with our joining in full knowledge of each other, a strange and blessed thing occurs. We are not like dark wolf and light, but more like wolf and panther, or even wolf and rock, or wolf and tree. Mating in darkness, our child is human, with some unusual qualities. Mating in the light, because of the qualities of my race, a portion of myself passed through our eyes into you, and a portion of you into me. With this act, it is not my seed alone that enters, but my full self, to participate equally with you through the generations. We are not the same as we were, and this will become more apparent to you with each passing day."

"I already was different from the others," she says moodily, for their time of parting is near and she is sad.

"Very true: all flows according to its inclinations. There are other humans such as you, scattered beyond the horizon, but they are few. Your people have decided as a whole to encourage other qualities, like strength and daring, in a way you may find hard to understand."

"Like the way the herds decide to move to a different land?"

He smiles. "Very good. That is very like it. Dreams, and the inner vision, will fall by the wayside for a time. Always there will be a few people who dream, like you. But most people will choose to work with what's before them, will be entranced with objects, massive things and great deeds of war and exploration, with pleasure and cultivation of the body. The great objects and crowds you see in your dreams, they will exist on Earth as surely as the silent trees and great animals do now."

"Some of the things I have seen and heard are beautiful, and I would not mind living in those times. Some though are horrible."

"Each time you live, you shall choose the time and the place and circumstance most suited to growth and enjoyment. Each time you shall be different, and yet yourself, as each year's setting of violets upon the ledge outside is different, and yet itself."

"Why would I choose to live in a crowd, dirty and with sores, thin and hungry? I saw such a thing once."

"What, was it yourself you saw?"

"I think not, but a fearful, sad person it was...and I was very sad to see it."

He tenderly touches her clouded face. "Because of your nature, concerned as you are with maintaining a sensitivity, an openness to the feelings of others, you might find yourself in such circumstance to be in position to help them with your understanding and your love. Should you stray too far in sensual indulgence, a temptation for your nature as well," and he drifts a finger down to run through the hairs on the cleft between her thighs, making her giggle, "you may need to dwell once or twice in such a state yourself, to remind you of matters of the heart and mind that you must not allow to fall behind. But you must remember, little one, that each time the keys for your redemption shall always be close by, and the doors to any cage you have made yourself shall open when you understand their use."

She sighs, grasping the contours of what he is saying. "I sometimes wish..."

He rests his hand upon her. "Speak."

"I sometimes wish...I were simply like the others. They do not care why a thing is, only for games, and food and mating."

"In the quiet of night, they have their dreams and wonderings too, and yearnings as strong as yours, only they cannot understand them fully nor articulate them. They shall recognize your wisdom, and in turn offer what they can to you, just as your people reward you now with respect, and the choice of food and mates. These are good things, are they not?"

She is silent, and a couple of tears slide down her cheeks.

"The only thing that cannot be chosen," Josef continues, "is to 'ungrow' what has grown. You have chosen, Tera, and you cannot excise what you know, although you can ignore it, to your loss. When you trust that who you are is blessed, no matter how unusual or momentarily incomprehensible, and you follow your own path, your own intuition and desire, then all that you are, and all that brings you happiness, can only multiply, and you will find treasures always scattered along your way."

She is somewhat comforted, but her grief is leading her on another tender path. She nestles her face into him, smelling him through her tears. "Why cannot I come with you, and be with you now and forever? You say I should follow my desires, and yet I may not go. The others mean nothing to me now..."

He strokes her hair, which shines even in the darkness. Their hearts ache as one, and will forever more: he has no choice in this now. "The day our son is born, shall you drop him in the wilderness, simply because he will venture there someday?"

She ways nothing, only sniffles.

"You see. This structure is for your protection, your guidance. This grief shall pass, and you will find pleasure among your days and nights again." Josef finds himself in the position of reassuring her of the same knowledge he himself struggles with, in the way of all true teaching. "Also you forget, little one, that because of your deed, I shall always be with you, and not merely the seeds of my race and being."

Her small sobs subside with this. "Our son..." she whispers.

"Tonight I lose this form and enter your womb fully as myself, only at the stage and in the form proper to fit within such a cozy space," stroking her womb again. "That is another advantage for you: where others must often struggle to find love, in each life there shall come a time when you and I shall meet, and in most of these there shall be recognition so intense, as to spark the way clear for all our subsequent path together. We may choose to turn away, of course, and yet the bond between us shall be of such potency, such undeniability, that, successful, we shall shine as example to others, a living testament to this present moment. There shall always come a time when we, as two beings separated by distance or barrier inconceivable, but drawn by the golden cord from eye to eye, from heart to heart, make the long reach, and touch fingers together, and draw each other close, and see the distance or the barrier turn to mist and float away. Tera, I have seen some of these joinings, and they are a sight to behold."

"Will you look as you are now?"

"Such a thing would not be possible, nor desirable. Each violet is a little different, even from the one growing in its spot the year before. There must be growth, therefore there must be change."

"How shall I know you?" She is sleepy.

"You shall. Sleep now."

"No," she says, rousing. "I can sleep tomorrow, when you are gone."

"Then kiss me..." he says, with a sudden passion, reveling in the taste of her tears, kissing and licking her mouth, her nose, and cheeks.

She responds, then pulls back suddenly, aware of something, surprised. "Are you...afraid?"

He pauses, but doesn't answer. He begins to kiss and grab her roughly again.

She gently pulls back again. "Are you?" she insists wonderingly, tenderly.

There is a great, still, silent struggle in him.

"Why?" she asks.

Again he cannot speak, but his hand absently and tensely working her flesh is answer enough.

"You are so wise," she wonders, "surely you shall always have things go along your way, even if you don't like us very well."

"That is where you may be wrong, Tera," he finally says in staccato. "I enter your reality not as god, not as Lumarian, but as human. Do you see? I shall be prey to the same fears, blindnesses, pain and struggle as any mortal."

She sits up, mortified, and it is several minutes before she can speak. "Why did you not tell me this?" she whispers. "Why did you let me see you, Josef? Why did you let this happen? It was only for me—my selfish..."

"No," he says, very sternly, recovered, touching her mouth. "You still do not see: I shall gain, I shall grow and benefit from this experience. Just as I would not perform an act against my interests, so you cannot take responsibility thus when it is not yours. Our purposes...blend with our love, do you see? From this dawn henceforth, we embark as equals, with conscious will bent to our own benefit. Each time we meet, however, any burdens we carry are lightened, any ignorance illuminated, any fears lessened, any suffering eased. As equals, do you see?"

She eases back down, full of thought, and they begin touching again, yet new depth and succulence are present in their movement and feeling.

"Josef," she says after a while.

"Yes, my love."

"I shall always love you. I am not bothered by these humans' foolishness—I give them what they merit. I know I am foolish and stubborn, but I am not afraid of them. I shall always protect you. You shall not regret loving me, I swear on the Mother. I shall never let them hurt you. You must find me quickly in each life, so I may protect you. Do you hear?" And with this, she is a woman.

"Protect me now, little one," he says, very moved. He pulls her onto him, wants to be smothered in her, drown in her passion. She is the Earth itself to him now, and she is very sweet in all her frightening power. He surrenders in a new way for them, and she takes him with new strength. "Take me to the end of our days," he murmurs.

"...and then shall we be one?" she moans.

"...and then we shall be one."

Twelve

She is full of dread, as if with child. This offspring is long-nurtured, and her nerves are shredded.

How can people live like this? she wonders, wiping her hands on her apron.

She checks her cupboards. She is well off; it is fear of what is outside that weighs on her. Fear of it breaking in here, and fear for someone she loves who is out there.

There is a loud knock at the door, a pounding. Her blood and skin freeze. She stares stupidly at the door. They would have no trouble getting in; why let the door be destroyed? She walks numbly to it and opens it.

They come in, big, hungry, tired, acting the way men do when they're over-excited. Dangerous, therefore, but human, after all.

Although she has never been with the enemy, she finds she knows what to do. She makes herself inconspicuous, but does not act frightened, does not even feel her own fright. As they make themselves comfortable, scarcely seeing her, about a half-dozen of them, she detects who is the leader, and meticulously carries out everything he tells her to do.

The place fills with heat, with smoke and the smell of sweat and various kinds of dirt and grime, with the aroma of her good food. She doesn't bother to examine her satisfaction when they eat with relish. There is some absent-minded groping of her as she moves about among them, but rape doesn't seem to be on their minds. Fear, defiance, good humor; if she were to show any of these, it would be provocative: simplicity is best, she knows.

Out of necessity she does meet the eyes of their captain. She has known immediately that should she earn his favor, she would not fare badly. She knows this incontrovertibly.

She drinks some of their ale: might as well. She tries to relax. There is desultory talk. They are winning, but they are very tired. Maybe they will leave her alone. She actually eats a few mouthfuls herself. She has been working hard.

They start to fall asleep. She feeds the fire: the more heat, the sooner they fall asleep. The food regenerates her. She makes places for them to sleep, she cleans up.

The enemy is in my house, she says to herself over and over. It seems unreal. What will become of me?

The captain is very handsome, very quiet. They obey him as unquestioningly as she, but they do so out of habit, not fear. He looks after them.

She wishes there were someone to look after her. Only weeks ago there was, but that time seems never to have existed. She thinks of her husband and feels guilty for being so cavalier about the captain with the green eyes and the bright red hair and beard.

She lets him look into her eyes from across the room. She seems to have no idea what she feels when she looks into his, she discovers. That is a lie, she realizes next.

She thinks she has succeeded in treading the line: not whore, not virgin, not bitch, not mother or sister. Nothing these men would be triggered by. Neuter. She begins to dwell on the possibility that they will sleep, that they've sated themselves elsewhere (her mind wanders numbly over the faces of her women friends and relatives), that the war would move on in the morning, and so would they. The village is lost: she doesn't have to look outside to see that. But the troops could move on. She could survive.

She curls up inconspicuously in a corner, behind the broom and assorted other objects. She looks across one last time at the captain in her bed. He is looking at her. For a few painful moments, she waits for him to gesture to her. She even knows how he would do it. But he doesn't. She turns away and dozes.

She sleeps lightly, dreaming of assault, but always awakening to the same quiet room.

With dawn they are too tired to even be surly. It is no time before they are gone.

They have eaten all her food, taken her money and few valuables. But there is little mess, little is destroyed.

She is still afraid to look outside. She is sick now, now that they are gone.

After vomiting and crying, she cleans the place, cleans herself. She hears things outside, but doesn't know what's going on. She gathers together the scraps of remaining food, fixes them in a halfway palatable manner, and puts them down her throat. Aching, she sleeps, dreamless.

The door opens. She is on her feet, her stomach clenches brutally. The captain enters, shuts the door.

Alone. He is alone.

She feels it is late at night. How long has she slept? She gets a hearty whiff of alcohol.

It is all very dreamy.

He says, walking wearily across the room, that they are stalled for some reason he knows nothing of. They spent the day drinking in the village. She notices that he is not drunk, though.

He begins to undress beside her bed. He tells her to come to him. She is appreciative of his slowness, his being alone. Besides, he is very handsome. She flushes and obeys.

He looks at her, touches her, kisses her. He removes her blouse, takes possession of her breasts sensuously, gently. She is extremely aroused, but too ashamed to show it, except in secret womanly ways.

He gently pulls her close, it is all very odd. She puts her arms around his neck. She is comfortable. It is all very dreamy.

"Your husband is dead," he says into her ear.

She steps back prosaically, as if he has told her of a coming storm.

She stands there, her breasts just hanging in front of her. It is idiotic. She doesn't have a clue what to do. How does one respond in a situation like this? She feels her mind slip out of her skull and filigree about in the air, then wander up the chimney. In place of a mind, there is a scorching agony roaring up from her stomach. Not sickness, it is more awful than that. It hits her brain, hurts it. But, she gets the idea that there is a little spot in the top of her brain that isn't filled yet. It is filling rapidly though, and she doesn't know what will happen when it is filled. She really, truly doesn't want to know, either.

He touches her breast. She pushes away his hand. He does it again, the way men do. He is acting like men do, other men. She pushes his hand away again, roughly. This, she knows how to respond to. This is a clear-cut wrong. She looks back up at him. The Enemy. He grabs her, and she thrusts him away with all her force, snarling. He makes a half-hearted grab, and she begins beating him. She beats his face, his chest, his arms. She does not hit his nose, his eyes, or his mouth.

Just as she grows tired, he pulls her to him and holds her very hard. Of course, she cries.

They stand for a while. She realizes her mind is back. All is lost. She is in a vanquished place, a woman who went from her father's house to her husband's. She had loved her light-haired, light-hearted husband, her peaceful village life with her friends and relatives, regardless of the fact that she had always felt she dwelt somewhat apart. Life alone was going to be very hard, very dreary. This man...

He beds her then, and she simply responds. After their first passion, she shuns him, but he gives her leeway, then quietly reclaims her. He is very different from her playful husband, but there is a pleasant ancientness about the way they move together.

The next morning, he talks to her. He seems to like her. She can at least respect him. He is clean, he is civilized, whatever the horrible stories about his people. With him, she would get food, have a future. A woman in her position, she would not be criticized. The quarrel between their peoples is economic, not ideological. It would be assumed she had been taken, anyway. He has left his weapon out, seems to trust her. She likes that too.

She is prepared to leave with him, to follow him in camp. But he tells her to stay, that he shall return for her on his way back. They discuss some details. He leaves his marker with her, to ward off anyone else. She feels sure she can get by somehow for a while.

By the time he leaves later that afternoon, she is used to him, and kisses him affectionately. She is calm.

It is a long-shot. He may be killed, she may be killed. He may not be killed, but not come back for her anyway. He may have lied about her husband. But she is calm.

He may come back for her.

She begins to straighten her house.

Laura opens her eyes and lifts her head. What a strange, long, rambling dream! She looks out over the garden, at the roses Paul used to tend with such relish; the reds and greens shimmer in the afternoon sunlight. She looks at the woods over the fence, half expecting to see the handsome soldier with the red hair and the wise, quiet manner emerge. Those eyes!

Laura never much got into the idea of reincarnation or spirit-worlds, even all through her long years of marriage to

Paul (she smiles at this). But she has come to treasure and cultivate her dreams for their own sake, and over the past couple of months she has had some great ones. This one was especially vivid. She wonders if that fellow ever returned for her, in the dream, that is. She smiles again, comically shaking her head to clear it. Although there was a lot of fear in the dream, or perhaps because of it, she feels rejuvenated now, glad to be no longer young and adrift, but safe in her lovely home. Technically of course, still Paul's home, even after his death, since Outsiders still can not own Insider property. Before, she might have been reminded of her persistent fears and convictions about the inherent instability and untrustworthiness of society, but it has been years since she entertained these thoughts, and today they drift off, disappointed, unsuccessful yet again in gaining a foothold in her mind. There was no vendetta against her, since her artistic message had always been one of understanding rather than revolution.

She looks down at her small table, and smiles in surprise. How could she not have seen! There is the face of the captain himself, on the card marked Magician. She had designed this Tarot deck at the urging of her students, not studying it much, just listening to the descriptions given to her by them, and drawing what the descriptions suggested to her, in the same inexplicable way she drew everything. This man's face must have been familiar to her from before then, from other dreams, perhaps, to have used it in her art this way, she thinks, tapping the border of the card.

Next to it is the High Priestess, in her own likeness. Some of her students had had misgivings about the daring, maybe even the disrespect, of drawing her own face as that of such a powerful "entity," as they put it. She had scoffed and done it anyway, and why not? She smiles. Secretive, smart, aloof, beautiful—how many times had she been described that way in the press?

Whom else could she draw as the Empress except that glowing woman she had grown to fantasize over the years as a mother figure to her? The face resembles that of Paul's first wife, but she doesn't for a minute think of her as Marta, just as a friend. Sunny and serene, she sits in a field. Laura looks into her face for a while.

She flips slowly and idly through the cards. She has never done "readings" with them, she leaves that to her young friends, but she does like to look at them. Especially recently, they seem to trigger fantasies and visions of particular potency.

The Devil—one of her favorite creations. A definite monster with deep blue skin and red eyes, still vaguely human, and its expression impossible to construe as purely evil: too much wisdom and gentleness. "This produces an unsettling paradox to the eye and sensibility," she quotes to herself, giggling to remember one of her favorite critic's quotes.

Strength (used to be called Lust)—a woman and a human-seeming wolf. The queenly woman looks haughty, yet her smile is tender when you look closely at her face. The wolf snarls, yet you see his tapering fingers, with the nails bitten off, stroke her bare foot. Laura gazes awhile at this card. Her eyes mist over: all the sex-games she and Paul had played over the years. Worked up a sweat, they had—there had been tears, sobs and screams too, moments when they had almost gone too far, maybe had gone too far, and held each other trembling in the darkness afterward. They had seemed hypnotized by the recesses and baroque contours of each other's psyches, and had never tired of blending imagination, passion and play with sex. She feels one of the strangely ecstatic floods of tears, sharp pangs in her throat, that have become so common recently: her grief after Paul's death had lasted one period of time, then was a time of great busyness for her, the true flowering of her career. Then she had missed him again, and began comforting herself with imagining him, as he had done with Marta. Now, over the past few weeks, there was a stupendous pain connected with him in her mind again, an overpowering yearning. She imagines it is looking forward this time, instead of back: she is old, and placidly sees that she is near the end of her life.

She continues to search. Three of Stones: her first exhibition. Anonymous, of course: no one would have come to see the work of an Outsider, not in those days. Now, half a century later, you can't distinguish between the Insiders and Outsiders, not among the young people who worked and stayed with her. The new laws were all the foothold Outsiders needed: soon, not only would they be able to own personal property Inside the Wall as well as a business, but the Wall itself would fall one day, she is sure.

She doesn't dwell on this too long. By the time the laws were passed, she had already made her peace with society and moved on. But her first exhibition, that had been frightening. In the card, you couldn't really see the faces of the nervous young artist and the friend standing behind her, his hands on her shoulders, but it hadn't taken her students long to put the pieces together.

Searching, searching...Six of Wands, another favorite. After word had gotten out that she indeed was the anonymous young artist everyone was raving about, the social controversies already brewing had a new figurehead. She was discovered to have a certain magnetism, and with Paul's shrewd management she had trod the fine line between society favorite and society scapegoat. The tumult went on around them, but most of their personal experience was psychological. Her terrors reached a screaming new high almost immediately (Nine of Swords, she remembers, although she can't locate the card at the moment), then came a time when Paul forced her to realize that she must choose again, between trust and mistrust of society, the way she had chosen between trust and mistrust of him. Deciding reluctantly that trust in her safety was the only alternative to insanity, she had begun serious work developing it. They had had friends, of course, and some of this new drugless medicine...but it was Paul all along, Paul holding her head as she vomited from anxiety in the mornings, who endured her stink when she lay about for days, unwashed, reeking of marijuana and thrashing around in some kind of weird, boomerang rage at her success.

Ah, at last: King of Cups. There he is, and this time the tears victoriously slam through her eyes and run down her cheeks with hardly a pause, even while she scoffs at her sentimentality: it is only a damned card, after all.

She looks into his eyes, and feels the warmth build up from her gut. She closes her eyes and beckons him, demands that he come to her, be with her, stroking her spine, stroking, stroking...

"Laura?"

She opens her eyes. The blonde girl sitting at her feet is so radiant, so perfectly light, that somehow Laura's heart seems to throb in tune with her beauty, like harmonics floating out over a musical chord. Big blue eyes, and there is a worshipful feeling in the way the girl kneels before her. One of her students come out from the house to check on her, no doubt. Laura can't quite remember her name, but this is not uncommon nowadays: her memory slides through her fingers like rain, and it doesn't bother her at all. So she just looks down at her, feels herself return the girl's excited smile. Everything seems dreamy in the wake of her emotion: the girl simply sits quietly, and finally Laura is moved to reach down and cup her cheek gently, run her brown old hand over the girl's soft hair, so fine and warm she can hardly feel it at all beneath her fingers. How long have they been like this, without saying a word, no need for them really...

"Laura?" She lifts her head—ah, she must have been sleeping again. She holds her hand out to the warm, brown young man who approaches. He leans down and kisses her, then drops cross-legged at her feet.

"It's beautiful this afternoon," he says, smiling, an ancient, gentle cadence suffusing his words. He and Laura have become close since he came to live there; it is his loving touch which keeps Paul's roses blooming now.

"Yes...yes it is, isn't it," she sighs. Things do seem to still be shimmering, she notices. "Is it only me or...does everything look sort of...well, bright, I don't know..." Her eyes fall back on his face, and then she looks again. His expression...

"Oh, I don't know...probably both," he says with a smile, and then she sees his face change again...he looks into her eyes, and there is an odd new serious line to his face, but what kind of serious?

"Had some good visions, have you? Some good dreams out here?"

She smiles, her mouth a stiff, wrinkling parchment. "Yes," she says. She has grown accustomed to his telepathy, but it's still of course rather amazing.

"That's good, that's good," he says, glancing around.

She looks at him quizzically. He'll tell her what's on his mind at his own pace.

"You been out here a long time," he says, and just at the last word, almost not there at all, his voice cracks a little.

"Robert, honey, what's wrong?" she asks, touching his hand as it rests on her knee.

Their eyes meet, and that soft light cheer of his slides easily into a strong, serious silence. For a moment they sit.

"You're an old woman, Laura," he says, rubbing her thigh.

She lifts his restless hand to her lips for a kiss. "Yes?"

"I had a dream last night," he says, and she sees the black tears begin to form, and immediately her own tears come. She is so sensitive these days.

"Yes?"

"I was picking up your clothes. You had...gone away, and I was picking them up to pack them..."

She is struck, frozen with sudden comprehension, everything for the past several weeks falling into place in one huge flash. Suddenly they are gripping each other's hands.

"I put them to my nose and I could still smell you on them..." and she pulls him to her as he sits, between her legs, and he begins to cry. "I know that death is a part of life—"

She hushes him and helps him to cry.

She settles back into herself. It is almost twilight. She'll go in soon, or else she'll get stiff. Robert would be back for her in a little while anyway. But feeling so good, so strange, she wants to savor a few more minutes.

Good, but tired. Her pleasant, dreamy apathy of the recent past seems to be reaching a new peak. Over and over, the events of her life pass before some inner eye; an inner projector seems to be playing all the time now, and she tunes into its display now and then. Each time things seem to make more sense. Everything is at once smaller, and more significant; more important, and less serious; inevitable, and miraculous; all-ok-with-her, and plenty-of-room-for-more, all at once. She hasn't done so badly for herself, she thinks. And yet, it was also all there from the start: her talent, and her need for its expression and for love, her stamina. A wonderful ease to everything, too bad she couldn't have felt like this more when she was alive...

"I do believe you're...mellowing!" Paul teases, sitting next to her.

She looks over at him sarcastically. He looks so good for a dream, glowing with health, his eyes twinkling and so clear that she can see the strands of iris, dark blue, light blue, dark blue, green blue, light blue...

"A bit late," he says, "but...you know the saying.."

"Mellow," she mutters. "Easy for you to talk about mellow—"

"Yes, and easy for you as well, looks like," he says, and their smiles look like twins.

A part of her mind peeps at what may be transpiring, then pulls back in. Easy now...time to be delicate...

"I miss you," she says, and feels the emotion return almost as a result of what she said. She is a little afraid of it, with him beside her like this...

"I know," he says, and takes her hand. How warm he is! and that warm feeling that usually originates in her womb now seems to suffuse her from everywhere at once.

She looks at his hand. It looks in every detail like his hand, little marks and lines she hasn't seen or thought about for twenty years but recognizes instantly. She looks over at him. His face...

"I love you," she says, and the old tears start to stream, this time like there's no end to them, but they feel oh, so good...

"I know," he says, and pats her hand.

"I'm...tired of missing you," she says. I'm coming unglued, she thinks, feeling strange and trembly.

"Not much longer, now," he says tenderly.

She pulls herself together, a little scared. She looks out into the woods. "Who was that man, that man with the red hair?" she asks, not wondering why she would think he would know.

"Well, that's not the easiest thing to explain, especially to you," Paul says, and they exchange a look, one of their looks. "He's a part of you, but himself as well, just as you and I are a part of each other, but ourselves independently as well. The dream was sort of your interpretation of a process the two of you needed to complete, a part of the process you're going through now."

She squints and nods faintly, the way she does with him and his outlandish notions. Scanning the trees. "Process. When Robert was here today, we..."

"Yes..."

He never would help her out. "We seemed to...he seemed to think...he had this dr..."

Paul lays his hand on her knees. "You said your good-byes," he says at last.

"Yes," she breathes with an amazing relief. "I...guess..."

"There is no hurry, of course," he says slowly. "Would you like to linger a few days more? You probably won't be returning again, you know..."

She looks at him then, and finally, with acceptance, the feat she dreaded is faced—and is gone, a puff of smoke. He stands now, and his eyes are cathedrals. She wonders that she must have slept out here all night, because the sky is bright blue again. Goodbye, bright blue sky.

"Don't leave me again, Paul," she says calmly, and holds onto his hand.

"Come along then, my dear, it's only a few steps more."

"But...I can't move."

"Yes you can...it's a subtle thing but you'll manage it. There now, just step out..."

She feels a little rip deep inside, like when she lost her virginity, and then rises without difficulty. Amazing, the lack of stiffness...she raises her arms and puts them around Paul's neck, feels his big strong ones wrap around her. Up she flies into the cathedral as they look into each other's eyes, a bird darting from brightly stained window to white, flipping here, flapping there, to rest on a ledge scanning the country outside briefly, before ruffling its feathers in the breeze and taking off...

Now much later, Robert steps close to her chair. A gust of wind scatters the cards, and as he bends to gather them, for they are very precious, he sees some of them suddenly catch in a whirlwind, spiral up and up, and disappear into the night trees. He stops gathering then, knowing a signal when he sees one. They can reclaim whatever the trees have left for them in the morning.

He sits and buries his face in her lap. He finishes his first day's mourning in about an hour, then carries his beloved back to the house.

The End